I0659582

2014

Writing from Inlandia

An Inlandia Institute Publication

Editorial Board

2014-15 Workshop Leaders:
Corona: Matt Nadelson
Idyllwild: Jean Waggoner & Myra Dutton
Ontario: Charlotte Davidson
Palm Springs: Alaina Bixon
Riverside: Jo Scott-Coe
San Bernardino: Andrea Fingerson

Publications Committee:
Lavina Blossom, Julianna Cruz, Charlotte Davidson, Timothy Green
Judy Kronenfeld, Glenn Williams, Lawrence Eby

Executive Director
Cati Porter

Original Cover Design
Julie Frenznick

Book Layout & Design
Lawrence Eby

ISBN 978-0-9839575-9-1
© 2014 The Inlandia Institute and individual authors.
All rights reserved. All rights revert to author upon publication.
No part of this book may be reproduced without permission of the authors.

Welcome to Writing from Inlandia!

This book contains windows into the hearts and minds of Inlandia's writers - writers who have spent the last year working closely together to produce the poems, essays, and stories that you see here. This is the fourth anthology in a series that we expect to continue for years to come.

Writing from Inlandia is an anthology of work by writers participating in Inlandia's Creative Writing Workshops program. This year's anthology contains work from five different locations: Corona, led by Matt Nadelson; Idyllwild, led by Jean Waggoner & Myra Dutton; Ontario, led by Charlotte Davidson; Palm Springs, led by Alaina Bixon; and Riverside, led by Jo Scott-Coe; a brand-new sixth location, San Bernardino, led by Andrea Fingerson, has been working hard and will be eligible to submit work for the 2015 anthology.

The Creative Writing Workshops began in Riverside the summer months of 2008 with a single workshop in at the Riverside public library, led by Ruth Nolan. Over these past seven years, the workshops program has grown wildly. We are proud to call each of these writers Inlandians, and revel in their success.

Appreciation

This anthology would not exist without the talented and dedicated writers and workshop leaders who participate in Inlandia's Creative Writing Workshops Program, a sampling of whom appear here. It is only because of their hard work, and the time and dedication of Inlandia's Publications Committee members and volunteers, that this anthology was compiled, formatted, proofread, proofread again, submitted for review by the writers themselves, corrected, reviewed again, and then finally submitted for publication. Without that time and dedication we would have nothing to show for a year of good, productive writing—except, of course, the writing, which, thanks to all of them, you can now read here.

Inlandia's Creative Writing Workshops Program, related events, and annual publication of the Writing from Inlandia anthology are made possible by grants from the E. Rhodes and Leona B. Carpenter Foundation, the City of Riverside, and Poets & Writers Readings/Workshops Program, with particular thanks to the director of their west coast office, Jamie FitzGerald Lahey, and the James Irvine Foundation, funder of Poets & Writers Readings/Workshops Program. We also wish to thank Inlandia's members and the readers who make this anthology worthwhile. All of these sources contribute to the production of this anthology.

We also wish to thank our host venues for allowing us to use their space to hold our workshops: the Smoke Tree Racquet Club club house in Palm Springs, the Riverside Public Library downtown, the Corona Public Library, the Idyllwild Public Library, the Feldheym Library in San Bernardino, and the Ovitt Family Community Library in Ontario.

Inlandia is grateful for all of your support.

—Cati Porter, Executive Director

Contents

2014

Writing from Inlandia

Dedicated to Mike Cluff
1956–2014

Dear Mike:

In memory and honor of the late Michael J. Cluff

You were phosphorescent. The day was so beautiful, it seemed almost a sacrilege when I received the news. The weather gave the phone call a clarity I could not quite comprehend. Has it really been seventeen years since we first met? I remember my baby steps into the poetry scene. Your approval mattered.

You were fluidic. I blinked and my first book was published. You honored me when you asked me to feature at my first Inland Empire venue, "Jitters", in Corona, Ca. With the quiet encouragement of your students in the audience, it was a relaxing, intimate night. It lit my future literary journey.

You were magical. I disappeared and nearly ten years would pass before I would return to the literary circuit. My fight with cancer finally done. You welcomed me.

You were mercurial. We became closer in so short a time. More. Sharing memories of literary venues and performers long gone. During my re-entry into the poetic atmosphere, we discussed creative writing strategies. We bonded over the renaissance of performing and publishing poetry.

You were quintessentially unique. You honored me, becoming the first poet I published in my fledgling literary series. You saw the vision of my featured reading venue. Somehow, you and I had come full circle.

You are eternal. Sparrow-song woke me this morning, after days of crow calls invading my blessed silence. This last week was a rolling, thunderous mass of nerves, memories, and sorrow. I am struggling for the words to truly express the depth of your loss on my mother, me, your students, friends, and the world at large.

I have come to simply realize this immutable fact: There has never been an artist like you. There will never be another artist to compare to you.

Certainty

Imagine what it's like to be tethered to an IV. Dragging your IV pole alongside you, like all of the baggage you're afraid to leave behind. For a time, neither brave or well enough to go "outside", I would walk near the elevators and imagine a taste of my beloved ocean on the breeze blown through the main entrance sliding doors.

Once, resting in the visitors' area of the Urgent Care unit with my mother, a priest came by and asked if I would like for him to pray with me. Sitting there, feeling the air conditioning on my bald head through the hat I'd crocheted, I looked up wearily at the priest.

Taking in his heavily wrinkled, sweat stained frock, unshaven chin, bloodshot, red-rimmed eyes, wild, greasy hair and his reek of fear, despair and old liquor; everything about him cried, 'I've abandoned all hope.' As he reached for my hand, I asked, "Are you okay? Do you need a moment? Would you like to rest beside me?"

Perhaps I started to guide him towards me. I really don't remember. What I do remember is his expression which was so naked, I imagined his despair ran much deeper than he possessed words to express. He met my eyes with such need, a sob escaped from his lips before he could suppress it. Without a doubt, I knew how he felt. I'd spent too many years hearing too many confessions as a social worker.

He clasped my hand like a lifeline. I was dying. I'd been too sick too long. However, what strength I had remaining, I gave it to the priest--without reservation, without hesitation. My eyes met his. "It will be okay," I told him. "Everything will be okay. This I know. This I promise you." My words ringing with the fever of certainty only those who are dying possess.

"Celena?" My mother looked up from her sketching beside me. Noticing the beleaguered condition of the priest, she drew a protective arm around me. I held determinedly to the priest's hand. My strength a fraction of what it had once been.

"Celena." This time a statement from my mother. I sighed. Willing her to understand, I couldn't die anymore than I was already dying.

""Everything will be okay," I murmured to the priest. Holding on with the last of my strength. "You will find peace. This I promise you."

The priest closed his eyes for a moment. His lips moved in silent prayer. The pain left his face for those few fragile seconds. For a moment, he looked almost beautiful. Radiant.

Opening his eyes once more, the priest's eyes met mine with renewed purpose. Peace. He shared the prayer he had offered me earlier and gave me a rosary. Then he walked unsteadily away--down past the nurses' station to the other patients waiting for him in Urgent Care.

First Contact

(Modern Love I.E. to O.C.)
For S.

Last night when we spoke you mesmerized me, my sorcerer
your words like splashes of water into my cupped dry hands
greedily swallowed into my parched throat
I opened my mouth to speak, my eloquence had escaped me
struggle though I did with words
It was like a dolphin wrestling an owl
The wisdom tempered by the intellectual play
Our contrasts make us a formidable mirror

I don't believe in coincidences, my sorcerer
Perhaps we cast the same spell into the Pacific
and the Fates saw fit to wash us upon the same shore
I only know when I looked up I found your compelling blue
        eyes
And recognized something with those depths
Has it been less than 3 days?
Each day I feel I have known you that much longer, much
        longer than days can contain

But time does not fly on the back of your wings, my Golden
        Eagle
Time flies and soars and circles in graceful dips, swirls, turns
        and dives
I know in my heart you were looking for me, my hunter
And I, Diana, Goddess of the Hunt, became a captivated prey
This white rabbit, diving dolphin, silent wildcat if you will

Saw you
Something within you made me stop pacing and slowed my

whirlwind of a mind
calmed my whirlwind of a mind

Your first touch. A hand on my shoulder, from your lips "Did
        you recognize me too?"
And though we orbit one another within the swirling mass of
        our lives
Still we reach out, sure fingertips touch solid fingerprints
Indelible your fingers sparked a fire crackling with my
        lightning touch
Pure hot energy to pure cool energy
And suddenly I lost my momentum

The Story Stutters

The white rabbit on her screen saver mocked her. Wryly, she thought of her abandoned storyline; the girl who became a rabbit who became a machine. Next to her bed lays a small clear topped purple box. Inside the box is fragments of poetry--pieces of ideas. Most nights she sits quietly staring at the box for inspiration. She's stopped recording her thoughts on lined paper. The story of her white rabbit has refused to follow any form. Now she draws pictures and diagrams of rabbits and foxes. They whisper their tales into the midnight wind.

Celena Diana Bumpus

For Nour

(Riverside, Ca., USA to El Obour City, Cairo, Egypt and Back)

Your last words to me as I hugged
you "goodbye" in front of my home
in El Obour City, Cairo, Egypt,
I don't remember. What I remember
is how much I had come to love you
as a mother-in-law. How close
we had become during my three months,
in Egypt, married to your son. I
remember how you took care of me.
Tried to show me how to be a proper
Egyptian wife. I remember our
playful argument about my refusal
to cook. How you kept reminding me,
"In the USA you are going to have to
cook for your husband. Not your
mother." I remember you feeding me
more food than your eldest son, while
teasing me about my "American" weight.
I remember how much I loved the cakes
you made. You showed me how to
make the perfect tuna fish for the lunch
we shared on the Persian rug, you gave
us, on the floor of my living room. I
remember you encouraging me to have
lots of babies--you couldn't wait to spoil.

Celena Diana Bumpus

Just...Hey

Been working since 5:30 a.m.
If I could shove a nail in between my eyes
and hammer into my thoughts
I would gladly release them
Instead I am bound by the confines
of this weak body
these wild notions
and those good intentions

I am growing weak
my strength leeching away
like so much breath through my lungs
and I don't know how to slow down
I've got too much to fit into
one solitary day

I have become reckless with my health
overextended and bent over with
these runaway ideas
I am hobbled by my own fatigue

Pull it together
I've been pulling it together so long
I am being pulled apart
I am like taffy
Though most see me as a bending tree
Somewhere I find strength
so many caring people
my concerned students

to sustain me
They pick up my gloppy strands
cradle me inside their hands
and say, "I see you. You are here with me now.
Its okay. I will be be the wind with you.
I will be that uplifting breeze
that will set you down gently."

Celena Diana Bumpus

Late Night Succor

For S.

I.

Late night succor in	slide of bow	spine arches
	meets every wild note	drum pounds
edges of songs	to contain	fire within
yet the music	fights	its careful confines
to writhe	dip	and reel
This is not a waltz	but music that	begs the
	glimpse of a	curved calf
	toss of	an untamed mane
	the curl	of an auburn lock
	over a dark	hazel eye

II.

It is here	within these	wee hours
brisk air	cooling	my infernal skin
I will dream	of you	most often
my sorcerer	with eyes	so clear they cut
the music	burst	inside my ears
the words	from	my lips and
find	themselves	without struggle
in		
between the lines	on	these pages

III.

It is here	I find how much	I care for you
all anew as	I discover	and rediscover
	all of the reasons	I love you
my Golden Eagle	so sleep long	my Golden Eagle
	and rest hard because	when we awake

there will be no rest
for the wicked and   sleep will be a mere
                          memory   again

Celena Diana Bumpus

She Doesn't Pout

She's more of an in your face kind of girl.
She doesn't grumble under her breath.
She meets your eyes with a defiant pride.
Daring you to even think the word "sass"
in the same thought as her name.
"Sass." Who uses words like that?
She doesn't sass. She tells you straight.
Take it or leave it. Like it or don't.
There is no defiance in the truth.
Sass be damned.
Pout?
Who pouts but women who have no confidence?
A child pouts. A woman makes decisions.
She decides what is not worth her time.
Sass and pout.
No.
Her parents raised her to think more of herself.
A thinking woman has too much going for her.

Deenaz P. Coachbuilder

a shroud for a butterfly

fine limbs drag
torn wings flutter
rainbow colors
reflect the glint
of the crystal
spring sun
my helpless tears
its shroud
on a broken
April day.

Deenaz P. Coachbuilder

My one regret,

I wish I were a younger grandmother
    by twenty years or so.

Not yet two years old,
    too young to remember me
after month long separations,
    we learn each other anew
each time we meet.

Each time a celebration
    of a new tooth,
a vocabulary of dada and mamma
    exploding to so many more,
the sturdiness of limbs that climb
    a gaze expectant with wisdom.
I remember the last time I kissed you
    and held you tight,
        now longing for the next one.

Insha'Allah,
    perhaps I will see you grown,
an adolescent, then a graduation,
    the first step into a professional world.

It is that time when the night
    crawls like a lazy caterpillar.
The cricket is surprisingly silent,
    dawn yawns and delays the sun.
The household hushed,
    I walk away unnoticed
towards the destiny
    that is reserved for all.

I do not hear the sound
    of the shifting viridian leaves.
The numinous moon kisses the curve
    of my pale dissolving shoulder.
The morning's sparkling dew
    soothes my porous skin.
The young sun melds my eyes
    into the evaporating mist.

I do not slip away
    into oblivion
 but will remain
    a part of this sacred earth
in the animals you pet
    the mountains you climb,
the oceans you navigate
    the soil you till.
And in you,
    for your blood is my blood.
Listen to that hummingbird--
    that is my heartbeat.

And when you choose
    to write a poem
they will say
    he reminds us of his grandmother.
In your spirit something of me
    will walk this land again.

Deenaz P. Coachbuilder

The tooth fairy

The tumult of the breaking school day swirls
through the halls of this alternate school campus.
Laurie, a young lady labeled "high functioning" calls out
"I'm assisting the handicapped" as she helpfully
wheels her friend's chair from the bus
into a specially designed class room.

Broad shouldered Tony flaps his hands held in front of him
as he saunters in. He can read, but cannot smile,
ancient wisdom lines his brows.
Some I recognize by the sounds they make
not quite words, but I understand.
Sometimes they let me climb into their world.
Sometimes theirs is a lonely fortress

Here comes Joe, running into the front office
from a separate section of the building.
Recently expelled for carrying a gun
in his worn back pack, he is on loan to me
for a precious defining year. Then,
he must return to his home school.

A six year old angel. Glorious curls, eyes with the glow
of smoldering bronze, delicate features,
a naughtiness begging to be noticed.

"My tooth is falling out Miss Mary," he proudly declares.
"Let me shake it," she says, and together they tug out
this beautiful pearl white milk tooth.

Mary, the clerk, seals it in an envelope.
"Place it under your pillow so the tooth fairy
can visit you tonight."
Unfamiliar with tooth fairies he is full of wonder.

I found him sitting on the cement curb
when I drove in that morning, parking
in the usual principal's reserved spot.
"I thought I had missed the bus, so I walked to school."
He had walked a long way.

We gave him breakfast, and then, a second breakfast,
before I accompanied him to his classroom.

Mid morning Mary and I realize our mistake.
During Joe's break, we quietly exchange the envelope
hidden in anticipation, within the turmoil
of his desk, before he can transport it home.
Inside this one is a dollar.

A while later the whirlwind visits us, first Miss Mary,
then he runs into my room, to share this unusual event,
  a gift.
I hug him.

It must all come out well in the end,
  it must.

That comfortless,
  Joe will learn to comfort his own.
That wordless,
  they will find a song to sing.

28

Deenaz P. Coachbuilder

Approaches

Dedicated to Michael Cluff, philosopher, writer, professor and friend, who begins a new journey

1

A mysterious subterranean pulse
connects the pattern of nature
of which I am an incessant particle.

My story unfolds.

The deepest waters of the Comoros
are indigo at night.
Gliding regally through the ink-black depths,
the rare coelacanth
hide in rocky caves and rise to the surface
in the dark,
unveiling their shiny eyes to the mute sky.
Slate blue with white flecks,
fish of ancient times,
with fins bearing the beginning
of human arms,
did this precursor of man emerge from the waters
to colonize the land?

2

Through the gravest illness, when each day
crept like a lazy century,
he brushed aside my tangled hair
and fed me tiny delectables,
this amore of forty years.
At night when I rest my back against his chest,

the universe in me is hushed.

3

His beginnings were announced in a grainy
black and white jigsawesque sonogram.
I placed my recorder against the speaker
in a cold hospital room in hushed anticipation,
to capture this grandson's sonorous heartbeats.
Then at birth, his slight weight lay in my arms,
the sweetness of baby scent
filled a thousand capillaries in my lungs
and there remains.

4

Now, the wager of every step
is a drawing towards closure.
Scatter my ashes so I can become
part of the air we breathe
the sacred earth we tread.

Something of me remains.

Carlos E. Cortés

The Boy with the Backward Baseball Cap

I knew it was impending
There was nothing I could say
I saw disaster coming
One hundred feet away

His baseball cap turned backward
His pants down to his thighs
His mesmerizing smartphone
Was the focus of his eyes

No sense of where he's walking
No idea where he was
His mind is on his smartphone
No matter what he does

"Distracted walking encounter"
Is what they call it now
Disease of modern living
It's presence makes me vow

That I will pay attention
I'll always stay aware
Of everything around me
'Cause life just isn't fair

When no one pays a bit of heed
To other folks around
Their minds on texts and twitter
They'll run you to the ground

So on that boy kept coming
No exit could I find
No doors or alleys anywhere
The world is so unkind

But when that jackass hit me
And knocked me on my back
He looked dismayed, but not for me
His smartphone had a crack

From falling on the sidewalk
His animus was growing
"You made me drop my brand new phone
You don't watch where you're going"

I lay there on the sidewalk
While he threw a dreadful snit
But I just smiled and looked at him
And didn't give a shit

Carlos E. Cortés

Breakfast in Sun City

Breakfast in Sun City
It's family time again
People coming from all over
Get together because then

They can spend some time with Grandma
Meet at Coco's right at nine
Have an omelet or a burger
Cup of coffee would be fine

At last I get a table
To watch the world go round
The mix of generations
From some tables, not a sound

A senior staring into space
A grandkid at his phone
No need for conversation
Just people on their own

It's lovely to see families
Get together now and then
That man's waiting for his daughter
Oh, she'll get here, not sure when

But she sure won't hold her smartphone
And everyone will see
That she smiles and talks and listens
While he tells her of the tree

That's just about to blossom

And the grass that's growing tall
He's sure he'll think of something else
If not, that will be all

Until the time, a month from now,
When she drives down again
To tell him that she loves him
And will surely ask him when

He's coming up to visit her
So they can have more time
They've got so much to talk about
While he's still in his prime

Of eighty years of living
Of eighty years of thought
Of eighty years of wisdom
Of things that can be taught

To all of his grandchildren
Who can learn so much for free
So much that can't be paid for
They'll listen at his knee

Of course the kids are eager
But fiddle with their caps
And even as he talks to them
They're busy checking apps

I'm glad that I was different
When with my family
And even as the years went by
Made certain I would see

My Grandma and my Granddad
Each time I went back there

Such lovely conversations
I showed how much I care

Then Granddad went, so Grandma
Lived alone amid their stuff
They'd saved and stored for decades
There was certainly enough

For her to tell me stories
I'd heard so many times
I feigned pure fascination
That's surely not a crime

One day when she was ninety-three
When saying our goodbyes
"Next time we'll go through photographs"
She looked into my eyes

But they came two days later
Paramedics took her in
She was gone before I reached her side
That's surely not a sin

I'm glad we talked so often
I'm glad we talked so long
I'm glad I listened carefully
I'm glad I heard her song

I looked around the restaurant
And as I watched, I knew
I'd been a caring grandson
At least I think that's true

Carlos E. Cortés

Constant Companion

I met my new friend at a rock concert in L.A.
He rode home with me that night without asking.
He crawled into bed with me without invitation.
He was there when I woke up.
He's been my constant companion ever since.

Mr. Tinnitus has been ringing
in my ears for twenty years.
He never takes a minute off.
I've pretty much learned to ignore him
unless something happens
   like waking up in the middle
     of an otherwise silent night
   like someone talking about their hearing
   like watching The Guns of Navarone
     with that ridiculous scene
     of German gunners putting their hands over their ears
     when the monster cannons are about to belch
     as if that would do one bit of good.

But Mr. Tinnitus really raises his level
when things get noisy, like during
   T.V. commercials
   movie theatre trailers
   amped-up stage musicals
   blaring restaurant music
   or when someone in the car next to me
     turns up the radio full blast
     not giving a damn about the ears of others.

That's the cue for Mr. Tinnitus to announce

that he's upping the ante on his ringing
and for me to tell him
that I don't care how loud he gets,
I'm moving on with the rest of my life.

Carlos E. Cortés

Mentoring

Today someone else asked me to be his mentor.
I said yes because I hate to turn people down.
However, I really don't know
what a mentor is supposed to do
since I've never had one myself.

In fact, in the good old days
we didn't talked about mentors
so I'm not sure if I'm supposed to be
   a role model
   a coach
   a cheerleader
   a psychiatrist
   an anti-depressant
   a pontificator
   a prevaricator
   a masseur
   a fashion consultant
   all of the above.

However, this does create a puzzlement.
Since
   A: now they say you can't be successful
      unless you have a mentor, and
   B: I've never had a mentor, then
   C: does this mean
      that I've always been a failure
      but just didn't realize it
      because I didn't have a mentor
      to point it out for me?

Laurel V. Cortés

Colorado "Quakies"

We fly in on G-Aspen Sc-Airways,
skimming fourteen thousand foot mountains.
Next day we're jamming down zip lines through snowflakes
at the glorious Top of the Rockies.

Back down to toast those "fourteeners"
at the toasty Leadville Hostel and Inn:
hot food, hot drinks, hot conversation,
overheated rooms, but a very cool place.

In 1927, when my Dad was nineteen,
freed from his job guarding the gold mine,
he rode up to this place with his brother Revel,
guiding his horse/friend Nellie.

Exploring fir forests, eating from the lakes,
the youngsters camped out with flora and fauna.
They laughed in surprise at the whooshing noise
of the tall shivering trees they'd never seen before.

A thousand triangular leaves shimmy and shake
in the tree they call "Quakie."
The sound of the Old West is in the wind
passing through those Trembling Aspens.

Thirty-Five Cents an Hour

Born in Omaha in 1939, I moved to Carlsbad, California at the age of three. From a very young age, two things set me apart from my peers: first, I went through school much younger than my classmates; second, I began a thriving career at the age of 10.

I was young in school because I started kindergarten at age four and skipped second grade. Being tall for my age, I fit in comfortably with my friends, and folks did not seem to notice that I was often the "giddy" one in the group. In 1949, when I was 10 and in 7th grade (with no allowance), I started earning my own money by taking care of other people's kids. During my entire five-year career as a babysitter I charged 35¢ an hour.

From the beginning I had terrific qualifications. With one younger sister and three baby brothers, I could claim great experience in feeding, diapering, bathing, dressing, rendering first aid to "owies," chasing and corralling, singing to, quieting and cuddling kids ranging from infancy to nearly my own age. I knew age-appropriate games and how to cook breakfast, lunch and dinner. (The secret to raising eight kids, as my mother did, was to train five girls before even *thinking* of having three boys).

I started my career by accompanying my older sister Gloria while she babysat, soon substituting for her regular clients when she was unavailable. My own clientele steadily emerged from word of mouth until I was turning away business. These early years of my life—including three formative episodes-- helped to forge my character.

* * * * * *

One summer afternoon when I was 10 years old, Gloria

asked me to take over one of her Oceanside clients, which I happily did because I needed the money to go to the Del Mar Fair. But instead of taking me to their house, the parents dumped me off at the Oceanside Pier and-- without mentioning when they would be back--took off with a couple who lived there. I was left with my clients' boy and the two rather unruly sons of their friends. Unbeknownst to everyone but me, all three boys were almost my age. My clients' friends lived in an enclave of 40-50 tent dwellings (situated under and around the pier) which the government sponsored for returning Marine veterans' families in the post-WWII era.

Tent City had a chaotic atmosphere, with piercing noise from loud music, shouting, beer-drinking, ball-playing and shrieking children. The parents had left me a bit of money for food and I had some coins of my own, so we bought dinner and I led the kids down the beach and away from the cacophony. We sat on the sand and I asked the two who lived there about their daily lives. Naturally, they told me their most dramatic anecdotes, until my fascination turned to fear for our safety!

As darkness fell, my anxiety level rose. When I saw the inside of their "home," the stark reality of their plight gripped me; I understood why the residents had to be outside all day. While the kids collapsed onto their cots, exhausted from the day's activities, I sank into a camp chair, kept awake by the putrid smell of the port-a-potty and by the loud, boisterous voices just outside the tent. My ten-year old brain exploded with impressions and exploratory emotions, as I sat there trapped until very late that night. When at last the two couples returned, I collected my $2.45 and was taken back to my safe haven with a scrambled vision of life.

* * * * * * *

The next year, at age 11, I found myself in a beautiful home owned by a sophisticated, middle-aged couple with three small children. It sat on a bluff overlooking the golf course at the Carlsbad Country Club, where the father was the golf pro. The wife explained to me that she had a thriving career but quit it when they could "afford" to have children--the first time I had ever heard of that concept. After they left, I reveled in the serene setting; in the luxury of the home, with its midcentury modern furnishings; and in the good behavior of the children.

The woman had carefully laid out the food to be cooked, but I froze when I saw a strange, large prickly green ball. I sat in front of it trying to figure it out—how to cook it; how to serve it. I couldn't imagine feeding those thistles to children! After preparing the other food, as the kids were busy eating, I picked up that green thing by its prickly leaves, scampered out to the top of the bluff, and hurled it as far away as I could. Did the mother wonder where the leftovers went? Maybe, but she never mentioned it to me. Later I learned that the green thing in question was a large artichoke!

* * * * * * *

After a time, I babysat often for two sweet children whose parents were a lovely, lively woman and her husband, a Captain in the Marine Corps. Also attractive, he was somewhat more reserved than his wife. Even though I was chagrined to learn that Oceanside girls charged 50¢ an hour, I continued to charge 35¢. But this nice lady usually gave me more than my asking price—what a treat!

After work one night, the Captain parked in front of my home to drop me off, took out the money his wife had given him, smiled at me and said, "If I told you that you have a cute figure would you hold it against me?" Although shocked because it was the first remotely personal thing he had ever said to me, I laughed, grabbed the three dollars, and stuck out my tongue at him. I heard him chuckle as I hopped out of the car and jetted into the house.

After contemplating this incident, considering what I knew about the man, and pondering how to manage our future moments riding together, I came to a decision. The next time he picked me up--while on the alert, of course-- I just chatted away in my usual casual manner. He seemed relieved. Our exchange kick started a joking (but not flirty) association that put us both at ease for the short times that we were alone together.

I was pretty sure that the Captain was not aware of two things: first, that this high school junior was only fourteen years old, and second, that my mother was a police officer.

* * * * * *

I never told my mother about any of these experiences; she had enough on her plate as a working supermom. But through these and other challenges and misadventures I had gained a confidence beyond my years. This self-assurance helped put me on an even playing field with classmates who were two or even three years older than I. Graduating from high school at sixteen and feeling the full exuberance of youth, I was not afraid of anything!

Don Dietz

A Beautiful Day Turns Ugly

Dawn was just starting to color the night sky. Soon the bright sun would peer over the San Jacinto Mountains. We awoke to a new day with the birds chirping, leaves rustling in the breeze and the blue sky. As usual Sally headed to the kitchen to start the coffee pot. I got out of bed, went to the kitchen and got the bird seed and peanuts. While I was feeding the birds, Sally met me on the deck with our coffee. Sitting down we began to enjoy nature's wonders. The Stellar's Jays and Chickadees came for their treats and soon the pesty squirrels followed. The smell of the pines and cedar filled the crisp clean air while a slight breeze rustled through the oak leaves. The sun was up and the bright blue sky completed the painting of this beautiful morning. We decided the day was perfect for a mountain hike on Ernie Maxwell. We have been to the trail many times but for some reason today we had trouble finding it and the parking spot. Finally, we spotted it and parked. Sally put on the backpack and donned her poles while I stretched. We looked at each other with the same expression remarking on the picture perfect day it was. Life is good!

Working our way along the trail we could see across the valley below as we tried to identify various landmarks. A feeling of wide open space embraced us. The air was clean and the smell of the pines and cedar was intoxicating. As we hiked the sounds of the forest were amplified in our imagination. The Seller,s Jays squeaked, the sound of woodpeckers in the distance and the caw of the crows were melodies to the ear. Stepping over and around rocks little lizards scampered back and forth across the trail occasionally stopping to stare at these two humans invading their territory. Farther along the trail beautiful wild flowers peaked out from rocks and climbed up coves. The quiet trickle of a spring could be heard in the distance. We rounded a corner and found a spring meandering down the rocks. As we looked up at the alcove of rocks a beautiful stand of wild azaleas captured our eyes. Out came the camera to record the flowers and nature at its best. We saw old tree snags laying on the forest floor while some remained erect and proud. Many trees have taken very interesting shapes as they reach for the sun, some twist, turn and bend in awkward directions. We were greeted by another hiker following a dog on a leash. The dog was greeted with a "Hi poch" and a pat on the head. There was movement in the brush. I stop and peered into the bushes where I saw a deer watching our every move. Sally approached quietly as I pointed it out. Then it seemed as though everything stopped, creating a strange, eerie feeling. Suddenly the ground rumbled and began shaking violently. I froze in my tracks. Sally let out a scream, "My God it's an earthquake." Trees waved relentlessly, boulders left their perches rolling down the mountain and old snags crashed to the ground. Rock and debris were crashing all around us. We thought, when will this mayhem stop. Please stop!

Finally calm was restored and my first concern was for Sally, where was she and was she safe. I was thrown against a downed tree. I was able to move and could tell that I had some bumps and bruises. I slowly got to my feet and began feeling a tremendous pain in my leg. It wasn't broken but my left knee was locked and would not bend. Through the cloud of dust I spotted Sally against a large rock a short distance away. I called out and quickly hobbled to her. She was dazed but appeared not to have any major injuries. She had bruises and scratches on her arms but otherwise she was fine. We sat there trying to calm down and gather our thoughts. How are we going to get down the mountain? Will there be aftershocks? Once down the mountain what will we find on the roads and in town? Will the cabin be standing and useable? Can we get there? After a few minutes we stood and embraced each other appreciating our good luck. The eerie sensations before the quake were gone returning the natural calm and beauty to the forest, although trees and rocks had been rearranged. We focused ourselves and found what was left of the trail. We began the painful hike down the mountain and back to the car. The rocks and downed trees created new obstacles which we had to maneuver until we reached the trailhead on the way to the car which was not damaged. After stowing our gear I asked Sally to drive as my leg was too painful. We didn't see much damage on the drive through town and back to the cabin, except for several old cabins that had fallen off their foundations. A tree had fallen on a house roof and there was only minor problems to the road. The center of town survived the quake with only some fallen tree limbs and broken windows. Starting up Highway 243 toward Pine Cove rocks and debris cluttered the road. There were major cracks in the road where it buckled and a significant rock slide around a hairpin turn closing one lane. Sirens could be heard as emergency crews were responding to numerous problems. The mountain disaster teams were mobilized in response to calls. Emergency electrical crews were attempting to restore electricity. Amazingly, all of the first responders were methodically performing their roles. We were relieved to finally see our little cabin standing undamaged.

Once the initial shock of the earthquake was over, a cautious normalcy returned to Idyllwild. People were helping people, debris was being cleaned up and broken windows covered. Word was slowing drifting in to the disaster center reporting damage and injury assessments. Much to everyone's surprise injuries consisted of only cuts and bruises and property damage was minimal. Considering the strength of the quake and the trauma it caused, we survived.

In a few days people will get their lives back in order and the

coffee shop conversation will change to sports and politics—
that is until the next big one.

Don Dietz

Taking a Hike in Idyllwild

Let's take a hike
Find a trail that's right
Through the meadow over the rocks so tight
It's into the woods so tall with bushes so small
We stop to observe birds, lizards and who knows what all
We hike on seeing mountains, crag, rocks and domes
That's Tahquitz peak, Suicide Rock and Lily best known
On the trail the oaks, pines, and cedars majestic, green and tall
Covered with a ceiling of blue
Clean, clear air breezes through
We sit on a rock to drink and talk
We marvel and think of all that surrounds
Observing natures finest sights and sounds
Up to the mountain top we hike
Now it's back down in due time
To reflect on today's climb

The Conductor

The orchestra assembles on the stage. Strings take the place of honor in the front, percussion in the rear and horns and woodwinds in the middle. A short warm-up commences. The Concert Master stands, faces the orchestra and plays a middle C giving the musicians time to tune their instruments. After completing this ritual the lights dim and quiet consumes the concert hall. The audience waits with eager anticipation.

The conductor steps to the podium and respectfully bows to the audience. With his baton in hand he turns to face the orchestra, gracefully nods and raises his baton. All eyes are on that baton as if it were a magic wand. The musicians watch for the moment the baton starts to move and at that precise instant the sound of the orchestra radiates in the great hall.

The conductor through his movements, facial expression, eyes and baton controls the tempo and dynamics of the orchestration. The violins, violas and cellos offer the listeners the foundation for the entire musical score. The horns and woodwinds support and compliment the strings adding expression (expressivo) to the piece. The percussion form a crescendo to emphasises a stanza much like the exclamation point to a sentence.

 He begins his orchestration by setting the tempo of the music. The initial romantic tempo (the robato) flows smoothly for a movement then a short movement (the intermezzo) changes the dynamics for several stanzas until becoming more lively and fast (the allegro) starting the second movement. The conductor gradually quickens the tempo (the acclerando) to a grand finale (the grandiso). The entire orchestra is completely involved. Everyone focuses on the conductor's baton as it carries out his exact desires.

The musicians read the notes on their sheets of music, but it's the conductor that brings meaning and feeling to the music through his emotions and the baton. As the second movement concludes, the finale begins with great energy (energico) gradually transforming to an lively fast tempo (the allegro) The horns and woodwinds express their dynamics and the percussions add their emphasis until the entire orchestra comes to the grand (the grandioso) finale.

The conductors baton comes to a halt. The concert hall erupts with loud applause honoring the maestro, musicians and his orchestration of the musical score. The emotionally drained conductor makes a humble bow to the audience. He signals the orchestra to stand to be honored. Tucking his baton (magic wand) into his pocket and he exits the stage.

On Fire

Late summer 1973, and everything was about to combust. She was at the Sacramento Balloon Fest, working with her crew to unfurl hundreds of yards of bright nylon when she heard a man shout "Who's the pilot?" His belligerent tone and manic energy put her on guard. His neon-yellow windbreaker blared MAGIC WATERBEDS. His thrust-out chest, jutted chin and corded neck radiated superiority. It was distrust at first sight.

"Jenner pointed me here." He gave a hard smile. "I'm Don Jusko, the sponsor. Who's the pilot?"

"I'm Judith Favor, owner and pilot." She extended her hand. He waved his backhand in a gesture of dismissal.

"Sure you are." He rolled his eyes and let out an arrogant bark of laughter. "If you say so."

"I'm one of the seven pilots flying today …"

"Don't mess with me, lady. If I'm going up in one of these things, I'm going with a man." He leaned in aggressively, probing her eyes, challenging her authority. She felt a visceral revulsion, a realignment of emotion from general distrust to specific hate. Whoever he was, whatever business he was in, this man repelled her. She knew about love but hate at first sight was totally new. She had to get away from him. Quickly she delegated supervision of the inflation to her crew chief and fled the scene. Her heart was seizing and she had to act on it, bounding across the dirt, pounding toward Wayne Jenner like a college sprinter trying to outrun her fate.

She was aware, for an instant, that she had wanted this to be a gracious morning, a generous morning. Diligent aeronautic training had prepared her to welcome a stranger into her balloon gondola. She also wanted to maintain her emotional cool but what she felt instead was apprehension, jittery nerves and a bewildering sense of repulsion. The combination rendered her nearly speechless.

How could she convince Wayne Jenner, the top honcho of this Regional Balloon Fest, that Don Jusko was not to be trusted? She had no evidence that the man was dangerous, just the roiling apprehension in her gut. But it was hate at first sight, and she was caught in it. No time to pause, or step back and observe. Her muddle-headedness was such that she could only eavesdrop on her own brain as it came up with nothing cogent.

"I don't want him," she blurted to Jenner, as he stood at the tailgate of his truck, writing on a clipboard. "You assigned Don Jusko to fly with me, but I do not want that man anywhere near me." She took a wide stance and jammed her shaking hands into the pockets of her jacket. Judith Favor and Wayne Jenner stared at each other's faces, studied each other for a long moment. She kept her gaze steady, her eyes level with his. "I don't want him," she repeated.

"Actually. " He stopped. Cleared his throat. "I can't do anything about that. What you want or don't want is your business. Jusko is a Sacramento businessman. He paid his money, he's entitled to his balloon flight. And you signed the contract. You have to give it to him." Jenner climbed into his Ford F150 and slammed the door. He did not look out the window.

She stood immobile on the sunburned grass, just to the left of his truck's rear bumper, tightening and loosening her fists. Trapped between responsibility and refusal. Blood vessels throbbed in her temples and throat. She smoothed down her shirt, the yellow one with the Sunrise Balloon logo printed over her heart, and smelled her own sweat. Metallic, the hot chromide smell of distress. Just one whiff of Don Jusko and she knew he was trouble. What did she owe him? How could she get out of it?

She looked across the field, wishing to see a woman who could come to her assistance, but that was futile. She was on her own, the only female hot-air balloon pilot in the state of California. Six male colleagues were busily inflating their own balloons and bonding with their local business sponsors, glad-handing and back-slapping. No help there.

On her way back to Serendipity a thought formed. *What do I hope will happen next?* It was a brief interlude of pre-occupation, mere seconds. *Safe flight,* she prayed, *safe landing.* Snapping back to the present, rejoining her crew, her gut seized. *Not diarrhea.* "Excuse me," she gulped, "I have to use the ladies room." Yes, diarrhea. Damn. *Not during the flight, please.* That prayer, at least, would be answered.

She drank a pint of milk to soothe her jittery stomach and supervised the inflation. She tilted the gondola and aimed the propane flamethrower into the wide mouth of the envelope held open by two leather-gloved crewmembers. She heated the ambient air inside it and brought Serendipity upright, her glorious six-story translucent cathedral. Don Jusko strutted around the perimeter with his perfect posture, shoulders back, projecting his voice as if he was boss here. How she hated men who acted so superior, so supercilious.

She confided her qualms about Jusko to her husband. "You felt this way last month in Chico, too, remember?" David sounded preoccupied, his gaze focused over her shoulder. She turned, too, watching their sons and friends keep the great balloon tethered to earth.

"I remember not trusting Doc Benjamin at first," she murmured. Her throat was dry. She sipped a bit of water, not too much because there was no way to relieve her bladder once they were airborne. "The doctor's intensity worried me. I wasn't sure what to expect from him once we were in the air."

Their gondola was small. The plywood floor was just four feet square, surrounded by aluminum tubing three feet high. With twenty-gallon propane tanks strapped into two corners, pilot and passenger had to stand very close. She didn't mind being near Dan, her instructor or David, her student. Judith and her husband co-owned the balloon but she earned her FAA certificate first and was now teaching him. Flying with an unknown man put her in a situation of forced intimacy. Flying with an obnoxious man put her in a frightening situation. Her moments of suspicion about Doctor Benjamin now seemed mild compared to her unease about going aloft with Don Jusko.

"And that flight turned out okay," David reminded her, absentmindedly patting her on the back. Three quick pats. She recognized his three pats as a sign of dismissal. *Yes, he was probably right.* The doctor in Chico had behaved himself during the flight and followed her instructions during the landing. Maybe someday today's doubts would seem equally silly.

She held her gaze on the job at hand, pulled her face into a stern expression. If Don Jusko looked her way, she wanted him to see her operating the flamethrower with confidence. A competent flight captain. Calm and cool. It was surprising to her, a woman who did not tailor her personality to fit the expectations of others, to suddenly feel so uncertain. She knew her stuff, of course she did, and had the FAA Lighter-Than-Air-Flight Certificate to prove it. She rarely expressed her fears vocally but her stomach told the truth. This guy was unpredictable. This flight could get tricky. She took three deep breaths to calm her jumpy gut and inwardly heard *Buck up, Judith. If you can't get out of it, get into it.* Just like that. She couldn't help grinning. *All right, then. I will get into it.*

She had fair skin with a constellation of worrisome blotches on both cheeks. Her smile had two stages, tight-lipped then hesitantly open. She aimed the second one at Don Jusko. "All right," she called. "We'll lift off in ten minutes and be aloft for an hour or more. If you need a restroom, now's the time." He gestured in his backhanded way, indicating he was above the need of such plebian facilities.

Pulling her spine up, stretching to her full height – taller than him by nearly an inch – she felt both brazen and giddy. "Get aboard," she said, voice charged with efficiency. "Stand in that spot and hold on. I need space to operate the overhead burner." The cocky expression on his face annoyed her, the fussy way he tossed back his long hair and preened for a buddy with a camera.

"What's that for?" He put one hand on the quick-release fitting attached to the hose of a fuel tank.

"Don't touch that, or the red handle above us, no matter what." Each word was sharp as a jackknife. His whiney voice annoyed her. "Keep quiet until I get the craft aloft and stabilized. "

"Ready?" asked her husband.

"Ready. "

She pitched her voice low and loud in an effort to get some respect from the troublesome male forced upon her by circumstance. "Hands off!"

They rose sluggishly into the hot autumn air. Surface winds were calm, too calm for her impatient passenger. Sweat beaded on her forehead, trickled from her armpits. She directed her gaze beyond him, glancing up and around, checking the cables and lines, taking in the quality of light. The Sacramento Valley sun was fierce, bleaching all color out of the broad rural landscape.

"Hurry up," he urged. "I want to win this race."

"Quiet!" She put iron into it. "I need to concentrate."

Once she had stabilized the aircraft at two thousand feet she turned to gaze at six brilliant balloons hanging stationery in the September sky. She explained that this event was never intended to be a race. It was simply a balloon fest, a festive gathering. She had said this before, but he wasn't having it.

"Go higher," he demanded, "so I can see better."

"Alright," she said to keep him quiet. *This guy is acting a little bit unstable,* she realized. *More than a little.*

"Go faster so we can win." He kept rocking on his heels as if that would increase their airspeed. She wished she could impose her will on the wind and get this flight over with. Being in such close proximity to this flashy, sarcastic male was driving her nuts. He talked constantly and fidgeted with the heavy gold chain around his neck. Every cell in her body felt edgy, on the verge of tossing the little prick overboard.

"Where's the finish line?" His tone was petulant. He hadn't heard a word she said. *What is up with this guy?*

Nearly an hour into the flight, no amount of maneuvering at different elevations had managed to move them far from the launch site. The small herd of trucks and trailers was still visible below. The shining width of the Sacramento River gleamed to the west. Then, around eleven, she had an inspiration. "I know nothing about you," she said in an inviting tone. Tell me about yourself." And he did, not chatting – for this man was incapable of anything resembling mutual dialogue – but he gave her an earful, a long rambling monologue about how he got into the waterbed business, how his business was booming, how many employees he'd hired, how many orders were coming in, how he was looking for a site to build a second factory.

Around noon she mentioned "The first tank is getting low on fuel. I'm going to do the switch-over maneuver." As she pivoted to the left to turn off the fuel flow she heard him boast "Oh, I know how to do that."

Before she could intervene, or even respond, the air to her right exploded in a solid wall of flame extending thirty feet into the sky, dissolving the nylon balloon fabric near it into gaseous vapors. *What had he done?* The idiot had disconnected a snap-release hose fitting from a full tank of propane, releasing gas under tremendous pressure and igniting the pilot light on the overhead burner. Used properly, the flame was directed up into the aperture to heat the air trapped within the balloon but this arrogant bastard had caused an inferno at the edge of the gondola, just inches away.

The heat was intense, the sound furious, the wall of fire overwhelming yet she instinctively knew she had to step into it to save their lives. *If you can't get out of it, get into it.*

"Move" she commanded, elbowing him away from the flames and moving into the conflagration. The only way to stop the erupting gas was to manually turn the handle at the top of the propane tank. As she worked, the force of the inferno scorched her hands and arms, burned her face and immolated the hair on her head. Once she cut off the flow of fuel, the blaze stopped but the pain was just beginning.

"What the hell were you thinking" she shrieked. Losing it, overcome with rage or shock, maybe both. The man who'd caused the conflagration was collapsed against the railing, speechless for once, vomiting overboard.

She wanted to do the same, collapse in a moaning heap. Her whole body was shaking yet she knew she had to regain control. *Willpower, Judith. Keep it together so you can get this aircraft back to earth.* The fierce fusillade had sent Serendipity shooting up to twelve thousand feet, more than two miles above the serene Sacramento riverbank where they started. She had trouble navigating the aircraft with half the nylon envelope burned away but what was left of the balloon shielded them from the direct rays of the noonday sun. *Thank God for a little shade.*

She had to keep her wits, had to bring the balloon down, had to find a safe place to land. Looking below, scoping out the terrain, she was relieved to see acres of broad brown fields stretching alongside the river. Winds were light out of the south. She let out a long, shaky breath. Good conditions. No power lines, no barns or farmhouses. She was reassured to see two balloonists already on the ground, four more descending. Her fellow pilots had viewed the calamity, of course, and assumed pilot and passenger were injured. Knew she would need help.

"Get me down," he whined. "I need a doctor. " He held out the backs of two hands, skin toasted into crinkles.

"I'm doing my best."

How long had the blaze lasted? Witnesses later estimated less than a minute, but the pilot lost any accurate concept of time. How long had it taken for the balloon to cool and descend? She could not say. Time slowed, sped and stretched between waves of pain. The altimeter silently marked their downward passage. Long, deep breaths helped her fight off nausea. The good earth came closer. Two aeronauts waved their arms, gesturing encouragement. A white ambulance approached from the north.

"Bend your knees and hold on," she coached. "Whatever you do, don't jump out until we come to a full stop. As soon as we get close enough to the ground, I'll pull the red cord to deflate the balloon. When I toss out two landlines the guys will haul is in."

Did he follow instructions? No. Her passenger bailed out, lightening the basket so she was carried airborne again. The scorched pilot had to make two landings that day while enduring the full force of the noonday September sun upon her third-degree burns.

"You the pilot?" she heard emergency medical personnel ask him.

"Nah, it's the broad," he snarled, gesturing toward her. "And I'm going to sue her incompetent ass, you can count on that."

Her summer day began with trouble, but where does trouble begin?

In the gut of the pilot, who sensed greater danger than she was able to describe to herself, let alone to the one in authority?

Did trouble begin in the attitude of a man who considered himself more mechanically competent than a trained and licensed woman pilot?

Did it begin in the faulty design of the Semco on-board fuel system?

Did it begin with Federal Aviation Authority for not catching the design flaw, for not issuing an Airworthiness

Directive requiring owners and manufacturers to correct the problem in present and future aircraft?

Or did the trouble begin in the rampant male chauvinism that permeated American culture during the Seventies?

The man who smelled like trouble continued to plague her for two years. True to his threat, the disdainful Don Jusko filed a lawsuit in Sacramento Superior Court. Luckily, Judith's balloon was insured by Lloyds of London, so she had competent counsel to guide her through the legal labyrinth. Aviation ligitation specialists filed a counter-suit. A team of seasoned Lloyds litigators researched every detail, and carefully prepared the pilot to give her testimony in court.

The arrogant bastard's lawyer knew better than to call Don Jusko to the stand. His blustering voice, swaggering strut and sarcastic superiority would have prejudiced the jury. Instead, his counsel called Judith as first witness and posed questions designed to discredit her. Innate shyness and dry throat notwithstanding, she told the truth of what happened on September 9th, 1973.

At the close of the pilot's testimony, His Honor called a recess. In a stentorian voice he summoned counsel, plaintiff and defendant to chambers. Closing the double walnut doors with an audible click, the judge declared "This frivolous lawsuit is wasting the court's time. Settle it here and now."

While their lawyers huddled around the judge's table, defendant and plaintiff were sent out into the hallway. She wanted to join her young sons but the bailiff prevented her from re-entering the courtroom. She avoided Don Jusko and he avoided her. Within half an hour, they were called back into chambers to hear the settlement. The pilot was awarded ten thousand dollars in damages from the man who caused the blaze. The arrogant jerk also had to pay court costs. Justice was done.

The burns on her body eventually stopped blistering and weeping but required months of medical debriding, cleansing and bandaging. Her hair eventually grew back. The scars on her face, hands and arms gradually faded from crimson to tangerine to white.

Never again did she pilot a hot air balloon. Over time she reached into the trauma as far as she could, putting as much of it on the page as memory could manage. The scars on her psyche still throb, forty years after being set ablaze.

Nan Friedley

Selfie

I tried to take one
but need a longer arm
to capture a face
I'd want to post:
as if taken from above
by a very tall stranger
to capture me
assuming the world is waiting

pressing the button
smiling for the benefit of no one
my image reveals
distorted crow's feet eyes
pie pan face, double chin
hair in disarray

        glittering beach in the background

a freeze-frame to show me
in a special place I'm not usually found
See, I actually have a life worth sharing
will others respond with a *like*
or even a *comment*

        how old do I have to be
        to no longer care?

Nan Friedley

Escargo Away

You are not welcome to
dine on my newly-planted petunias
gnaw daisy blossoms, chew vinca petals
leave me impatience
with a trail of gooey residue from
you and your slug brother

experts say drown you in cheap beer
rub Vaseline on pot rims
sprinkle coffee grounds
impervious to Corry's Snail and Slug killer
you linger
sampling my garden smorgasbord

searching groundcover for
your secret hiding spots
prying your sticky foot off my delectable ice plants
to gift you to my green recycle bin

karma will find you
sautéed in butter with shallots and brandy
            my pansies and marigolds
            wearing lobster bibs
            armed with tongs
            and two-pronged forks.

Nan Friedley

Browsing

Sitting at a nearby table I can hear them whispering
a couple in the corner booth at Chili's, middle-aged
he with a receding hairline,
wearing a skinny brown belt cinched under
an expanding beer belly
she with too much make-up
processed hair to cover the *mousy* gray.

Eyes fixed on each other
exchanging stories, pitching truths or lies
like trying on clothes at Macy's.
Are they a product of Match.com
a fix-up from friends, perhaps colleagues?
A surreptitious meeting?
An affair waiting to take flight or crash on the runway?
I can't look away, anticipating
what coffee and dessert will bring
a return to the rack to continue shopping
or wear home hoping for no buyer's remorse?

Nan Friedley

Not Worth a Hill

I picked at their coats
scooted them around
the dinner plate with a fork
tried my best to hide them
in my pile of buttered mashed potatoes.

Its pale green smile
laughed at me
while I attempted
various tactics
nibbling, swallowing whole
mashing into oblivion
dissolving in my cheek.

Sometimes they appeared in a medley
of corn, carrots, green beans, given the
odd name of succotash.
"Sufferin Succotash"
Sylvester must have been
a fellow bean hater.

I could still find them in the mix—
separating them from the *friendlies*
with my fork
leaving me at the table, sitting
staring at the offending beans
waiting, hoping I would be given a reprieve
from the kitchen table
but no, the pile just stared back

I decided my life was not worth

a hill of lima beans
so I ate them.

Nan Friedley

Highway Haikus

After midnight work
spotlights illuminating
CalTrans nightshifters.

Spectator slowdown
fender bender side show's on
coast by slowly…gawk.

Road hog threading lanes
claiming freeway real estate
leave us in his wake.

Corona crawling
inching rows of red brake lights
creeping parking lot.

15 , 91
an army ant regiment
merging from above.

Biker roaring by
weaving, lane-splitting menace
with inches to spare.

Nan Friedley

Let the Turbulence Begin

I'm D22
legs crossed, uncrossed
wishing I had a jumbo bladder
another hour and a half
to my connecting flight at DFW
too long

at least mine is an aisle seat
don't have to disrupt E22 illegally
using her cell phone or
F22 sleeping, drooling on the window

I amble to the back
rocking from side to side
glancing at fellow travelers
the lavatory door indicates *occupied*
so I wait between D36 and C36
I hear a snap
the window changes to *vacant*

a bearded giant zips up
as he steps out of the
pint-sized plane potty
I hover over the
metal toilet with
raspberry Otter-Pop colored water
not daring to touch the receptacle
dotted with pee

it's just about then the plane
jolts upward
I grab the safety bar
stabilizing my precarious squat
the pilot announces
please return to your seat
Just a minute…

               Ahhh, that's better.

Françoise Frígola

Mountain Fire: a personal experience

I can stop, at last!

For the last 6 days I have been chained to my computer keeping people informed of our situation, here, up on the Hill, where the Mountain Fire has been raging. I have been checking the relevant websites, kept Mountain Disaster Preparedness members up-to-date via our radio network, answered one phone call after the other, constantly checked reliable websites, posted verified information on the Idyllwild Emergency website and Facebook, did my best to keep people calm, reassured many, corrected wrong – often scary – information, posted the updates from WNKI our emergency radio channel, all of this working closely with Mike Feyder, the MDP president. Six days with little sleep of poor quality like all of the other eight MDP members who volunteered to stay.

People have been allowed to come back. I just finished helping organize volunteers for the check points on each of the three roads leading up to our village. This seems to be my last task. The reports over the radio network are that the return is running smoothly.

Idyllwild is coming home.

I lift my hands from the keyboard, remove the phone headset, and decide to keep the radio on, just in case. I lean against the back of my chair and take a deep sigh of relief.

Somehow, from somewhere, without having consciously thought about it, I was expecting that, once the pressure would be over, I would start crying – maybe from previous experience.

So, to my surprise, my chest first, then my whole body fills with calm positive sustaining energy.

I have a sense of pride as to what I just accomplished.

I realized how for six days in a row, except for a few hours of internal turmoil which I doubt anyone noticed, with little sleep, I remained totally focused, calm, poised, centered, sticking to the task at hand.

In all humility, I feel so good about what I have accomplished. I can feel it in my entire body. I stay with it. I want my nervous system to integrate these feelings of success, of peace, of a job well done.

Later, at 5:45 PM, I update the Idyllwild Emergency website:

After the Mountain Fire, it is with great relief and extreme gratitude that I return this website to:

NO EMERGENCY AT THIS TIME.

And I start crying.

******

Inner Crisis

Thursday, the day after Idyllwild was evacuated

Someone on the Mountain Disaster Preparedness radio network tells Mike Feyder, our president, that he was going to call him about an issue with Facebook.

I am not paying too much attention until, within a short time, at least three other people do the exact same thing: they all needed to talk to Mike about Facebook privately on the phone rather than openly on the radio network.

Facebook, for Mountain Disaster Preparedness: this is ME! Since Monday mid-afternoon, I have kept people as up-to-date as I can with verified information on our website and, especially on Facebook.

My body starts to feel threatened. I mean my whole body, which has endured so much physical abuse in my childhood, goes right back to these times when physical threats were almost constant; one "wrong" word, one "wrong" action and I knew I would soon be yelled at, beaten up, or molested. My body would pay the price.

Right now, my head knows better: there are hundreds of people discussing the Mountain Fire on Facebook. I am only one of so many and I only post relevant, verified information.

The little girl in me is experiencing this differently: it is me they are talking about, secretly, behind my back. I have to have done something wrong. I must have posted something I should not have written.

I continue to keep an eye on the posts on Facebook, keeping people up-to-date when I have new relevant information, answering questions, correcting errors, or scary posts, etc.

I doubt anyone can guess what is truly happening deep inside of me. Over the years, I have become an expert at hiding the deep inner fears I experience. But it is getting increasingly difficult to remain focused. My body is getting more and more tense. My solar plexus is totally blocked and painful.

I take a break. I go and sit on my back deck attempting to get into a meditative state. It does not take long before I decide to talk to Mike. I know he will level with me. But it is way too late to call him now. I will do so in the morning.

The decision calms my body a little bit.

One more look at Facebook. Not much is happening close to midnight. I am going to bed, hoping I am calm enough to get some sleep.

The next morning, after another semi-meditation, as I had promised myself, I call Mike. I briefly explain the situation and, in a few words, my childhood background which has been triggered, reason why I am having such a hard time with the knowledge of the phone calls he has received about Facebook.

Mike perfectly understands where I am coming from and re-assures me that the issue has nothing to do with me personally. He explains that the Fire Chief is upset about Facebook where many posts convey the wrong information, especially about people attempting to come back to Idyllwild when all the roads, including Control road, are still closed to incoming traffic.

I know I can trust Mike.

My body relaxes.

I feel much better.

The inner crisis is over.

*****

Praying for Rain

"Make it rain! Make it rain!" is the prayer I heard and read all over.

Praying for what is missing.
Some consider this as a "lack prayer."
Some prefer what I would call an "abundance prayer."

Prayers do not have to be limited to words. Creating an image of the rain and sending the image to whatever or whoever one believes in is also a powerful prayer.

The prayer I did repeatedly was to imagine my bare feet on the ground feeling the moisture, the water, the mud, and giving thanks for it.

My favorite, however, was the Rain Dance by the Idyllwild Art Academy students from all over the world. A video is on You-Tube (http://www.youtube.com/watch?v=nixWV_fT5IM.) One can see how much their heart is in it.
The comments are all positive, supportive, and appreciative, except one: "hey, ya never know, maybe this will work! along with prayer."

Someone totally missed the point!

However, regardless of the format, all these prayers for rain did the job: it did rain, just in time, and the fire was stopped.

But…

We got way too much water in too short a time.

As a result, we also got mud slides in the Apple Canyon and, among other flood damages, the Yokoji-Zen Center was devastated.

I strongly believe that our prayers were not specific enough.

If there is ever a "next time," let's be more precise.
Let's ask for just enough rain to stop the fire while keeping everything else safe and secure.

Lesson learned!

******

Michelle Gonzalez

How We Met

Not in your English 101 class
or anywhere else
at the campus you taught at,
but by chance
in an evening writing workshop
where the participants gathered
in a small airless room
in the basement
Of the library.
Coming often without
paper or pen,
as you enjoyed listening
to others read.
Somehow changing positions
from observer to facilitator
and one more time to friend.
But there will be no more
poem of the day
sent over email
stories from
the streets of San Bernardino.
Now there is only
an empty brown chair
in the basement of the library
where we first met.

Remembrance

One Southern California day, in 1962, a tall, gaunt man ambled through his worn, but tidy cottage.

In the past, citrus groves had surrounded the small cottage on its acre. Now the groves were gone. A solid row of ranch-style homes lined the street, and the old cottage looked like an early 1900's post card dropped into the present.

Robert Sutherland sipped his coffee, thankful for the morning caffeine. Then he sat the steaming cup next to the morning paper, on the simple wooden table, against the kitchen wall. *All of this will soon be gone*, he thought, with a hollow feeling in the pit of his stomach.

He was alone. He lost Margaret, his wife more than a year ago. Now it was time to move to his son's home.

Outside, the birds were silent in the gray winter morning, and the damp day made the warm kitchen seem even cozier. His stiff fingers turned the knob of his time-worn range; a flame flickered, then a blue ring glowed steadily under his pan of bacon.

Empty cartons were stacked in the corner, and the impermanence of all things hung in the musty air of the old kitchen. On the floor, a crate of well used hand tools he'd packed the night before, taunted him. He thought about his strong, capable son. *Won't need those anymore.* He frowned. *Rob has tools of his own.*

As his bacon sizzled, his eyes moved slowly around the old kitchen, attempting to fix the room's image in his mind.

His tired blue eyes reflected the emptiness of a pink glass cookie jar sitting on the green and white tile counter. A few crumbs remained at the bottom of the abandoned jar.

Margaret always kept that jar full, he thought, remembering the delicious aroma of baking cookies and the laughter of children as they ate the treats, fresh from the oven.

Next to the pink glass jar, an English teapot languished on the counter. He reached out with his finger and wiped the dust away from the hand painted violets on the china surface. His weary eyes moved back to the table and he imagined Margaret sipping tea as she had every afternoon.

He turned his bacon with an old spatula. The paint had disappeared from its wooden handle long ago. *How many meals did we cook with this?* He thought and knew the worn utensil would soon be tossed into the trash.

Most of this will go in the trash. He mumbled.

He lifted a heavy, black-handled pair of scissors from their hook on the wall and closed his eyes. As he held the iron scissors, he saw Margaret clipping colorful blooms in her sunlit garden, and he remembered her sitting, in the evening, weaving purple ribbon and lavender into sachets. The lavender scent still lingered in the kitchen. *How Margaret loved her garden*, he thought.

It seemed only yesterday Cindy, the neighbor child, was trailing behind Margaret in the spring garden, asking questions about each flower. Margaret enjoyed the child's curiosity and saved old seed catalogs for her. Then there was a divorce and the family moved away. *"Cindy'd be grown now; maybe she'd like Margaret's scissors,"* he thought as he placed the scissors on the counter.

He opened a cabinet door and stepped back to see the dishes on the high shelf. Yes, Margaret's favorite china platter and serving bowl, remained in their place. As he reached up and lifted the silver rimmed dishes, with their tiny, pink roses, tears stung his eyes.

Memories of Sunday dinners served on fine china, took him to happier times and soothed his lonely heart. *And she could cook too*, he thought.

He placed the china with the scissors. "Lady Jane will like these," he said aloud and smiled remembering his nick name for Cindy's mother, Jane.

Now, how could he find his former neighbors? Maybe his son would help him.

A few weeks later, on the other side of town, in front of a small group of rental units, Robert Sutherland stepped out of his car and carried his carton of treasures to a unit in the back. When he knocked, Jane Miller opened the door and invited him in.

"Hello, Lady Jane," he smiled, using the nickname he'd given her so long ago. He put his arm around "Lady Jane's" shoulders and gave her a little hug.

Wendy, an aging cocker spaniel, crossed the room as fast as her old legs would carry her, to see the gray haired man. He looked down at the old, black dog and remembered a young pup that followed him like a shadow while the children were at school. "It's all right girl," he leaned down and patted her head. "We're both old now." The happy dog wagged her tail and kissed his hand.

With moist eyes, Jane Miller watched her old neighbor pet the dog. "They say a dog never forgets a person."

Robert Sutherland looked up and nodded his head. Then he handed the china dishes to Jane. "Margaret's favorites. I know she'd like it, if you have them," he said.

"Thank you." Jane took the dishes. "They're beautiful. I love the pink roses. I'll think of you and Margaret whenever I use these."

They shared memories of Jane's children, as they sipped coffee in the small living-room, and recalled visions of playful kittens pouncing, in tiny jungles of wildflowers at dusk.

Then with his gnarled hand, he offered the scissors to Jane. "I want Cindy to have Margaret's scissors. Cindy loved our garden," he said.

Jane Miller took the scissors from his trembling hand

and promised to give them to Cindy.

Then she thanked him and waved good-by as the wobbly scarecrow figure of the once strong man made his way back to his car.

In his car, Robert Sutherland thought, *Cindy will remember Margaret's scissors; she'll cut blooms in her own garden now.* He drove away with a peaceful look on his face.

C.R. Hawk

Yesterday's Young Woman

Wrinkles surround her eyes. She brushes her silver streaked hair.
Like a threadbare garment, memories cling.
Frayed feelings must not tear.

A bundle tied with ribbon, letters read one by one.
Nature's canvas remembers.
Nothing can be undone.

Shadows in the moonlight. A moth around a flame.
She wanders in the darkness,
through a cold yet bright domain.

Jagged peaks shelter a meadow. Monk's Hood blooms in strong sun.
Hidden frogs call in the darkness.
Veiled poison spares none.

Mountain pines glimmer in sunlight. Coral bells lie at her feet.
Warmth caresses her wide-eyed young face.
One moment, in time, complete.

Soothing song of the ocean. The calm of a gentle embrace.
Seagulls soar above.
Sanderlings scurry in haste.

Yesterday's young woman is welcomed. Timeless treasure is found,
Embers of spirit rekindled,
And crumbling chains unwound.

Time deepens colors and feelings. Old regrets fragment and fall.
Sunrise paints a fresh portrait.
Nature replenishes all.

Ageless Vanity

It was morning and the woman was just sitting down with a cup of coffee to read her email. Oh this is interesting, exclaimed the woman to herself. I have been invited to attend my 60th high school reunion next month. She quickly checked her calendar to see if the date was available. It was to be a luncheon. She recalled the 50th reunion had been a three day affair with cocktails, dinner, tours of the high school and a cruise around the bay. She thought this one sounded more manageable. Later that afternoon she was talking to her neighbor. Guess what, I am going to my 60th high school reunion. The neighbor who was a decade younger, replied,"And how many are left in your class?" This was not the answer the woman was hoping for, but she took it in stride. However, it did make her wonder if she really looked that old. The woman began thinking. How can I look younger? I do have a whole month to ready myself for the big event.

So the woman sat back down at her computer to make a list. First on the list was to buy a new very modern sheath-type dress. Now in order to fit into such a dress she needed to loose 10 pounds mostly around the hips and stomach. So the next two items she typed on the list were, going on a diet and joining a gym. That seemed enough for right now. She immediately went on line and found a sensible diet she could live with and a gym nearby. That afternoon she headed to an expensive boutique and bought the dress, shoes to match and just in case she didn't loose all those extra pounds, a form fitting undergarment called a spank. Trying this contraption on in the store's dressing room was somewhat demeaning. She felt like a sausage being squeezed into a casing, but it did the trick, and she was able to get her new dress zipped up with the help of the saleslady.

The next morning she had an appointment with a personal trainer at the gym. He sized the woman up and started her on some machines, then some weights and also suggested she walk two miles each morning and take a step aerobics class in the afternoon. If you do these things I am sure you will meet your goal he said to the woman.

After the workout and the aerobics class, the woman practically crawled to her car. Once home she went into the bathroom cabinet and reach for the bottle of aspirin. As she carefully closed the cabinet an image appeared in the mirror. Heavens, who is this person said the woman knowing full well who it was. So back to the computer she went. This time she looked up plastic surgeons. There were many kinds of facelifts: the invasive, non-invasive, and the liquid kind where botox and hyaluronic acids were injected into the skin. The worst sounding one was jaw line reconstruction that had something to do with harvesting the fat in your neck to implant in your cheekbones. These all sounded horrible to the woman and be-sides the procedures all started at $7,000 which was out of her price range.

The woman went back to the mirror. "Mirror,mirror on the wall what can I do to look younger?" And the mirror an-swered, "Go back to the Internet and find a spa." So the wom-an looked up a nearby spa. The next day she took a two mile walk but instead of going to the dreaded gym, she went to the spa. First she had a deep tissue massage followed by a facial, a pedicure and a complete cosmetic makeover. Eyebrows were plucked, and her nails were painted a luscious red to match the red panel in the dress and the new red shoes. The makeup artist applied a light tan foundation to her face along with eye shadow, a swipe of rouge and rose colored lipstick. When the makeover was done, the woman was handed a mirror. The woman looked in the mirror and said," Mirror you were right all along. I may look my age, but I look darn good for my age."

The day before her reunion, the women went back to the spa for another complete treatment and makeover. She had lost 5 pounds by walking every morning, and she could zip up the dress by herself. She was ready to face her high school classmates.

Sally Hedberg

What Defines A Favorite Place?

When discussing the topic of travel invariably this question is asked, "In all your travels what is your favorite place?" This is a very hard question to answer if one has traveled extensively. There are many historical and natural places that I have enjoyed visiting. Destinations listed in wonders of the world, the book "100 Places to Visit Before You Die," the National Parks all over the world come to mind. Cruises, hikes, people, foods, smells, oceans, lakes, volcanoes all swirl in and out of my brain. "So I ask myself where is my favorite place or places?" To help me answer this question I defined the elements of my favorite place.

I treasure remoteness from the busy world, but I want to be surrounded by friendly people. I like eclectic music; drums, clarinet, guitar, didgeridoo, gut bucket, conch shell, bird songs and the mournful sound of coyotes. Scenery heightens my sense of awareness. Visions flash before me like the clicking of a camera. I see dwellings; RV's, tents, yurts, hostels, motels, hotels, and bed and breakfast inns. I smell muffins in the oven and bacon and eggs on the stove, and the fish and seaweed in the ocean. I taste the sweetness of a juicy peach and a fresh pineapple. Leafing through many travel articles and books, I find my favorite places are rarely mentioned.

My number one favorite place is Idyllwild, California. My husband I have enjoyed the summers here just one hour away and 20 degrees cooler from the oppressive 100 plus degree weather at our home in the desert. We discovered this perfect little hamlet in the San Jacinto Mountains six years ago and continue to relish our summers in this cozy town nestled in the pines. The mountain folk surround us with love like they have known us forever, and melodies fills the air everywhere you go. We spend a great deal of time just sitting on the deck watching the sun come up over the mountain and feeding peanuts to a variety of birds. After dinner on the deck we watch the orange-pink Alpine glow on Tachquitz Peak and Lily Rock. All our home cooked meals are eaten outside. The exception being when we go to the many superb restaurants in town. Fast food franchises are not allowed on the mountain, and the friendly little market has most everything we desire.

When we tell our friends how much we like Idyllwild, they in veritably ask, "What do you do up there?" Sometimes its hard to describe the euphoric feelings one gets hiking up the mountain trails, or seeing wildflowers, hearing song birds, watching squirrels chase each other, or just looking across the valleys beyond. I realize not all will respond the way I would like them too, and it makes me sad. But that is only because I love Idyllwild so much.

Is it possible to have another true favorite destination? I didn't think so until I visited Molokai, part of the Hawaiian Islands. I had always been fascinated with this small remote island in the Pacific. Molokai was the first Hawaiian island to be inhabited by the Polynesians. They arrived in canoes to the area called Kalapapa which later became home to the dreaded leprosy colony now a National Park.

There is very little about Molokai in the travel literature except that the locals do not encourage visitors. When I thought about my criteria: remoteness, friendly people, scenery, music, food, and shelter, it was worth a visit. We took the 90 minute ferry from Maui to the pier at Kanakakai, the only real town on Molokai. The small rental car was waiting for us at the pier with keys under the mat. We thought the locals were very trusting until we realized there weren't many places to go. There are no stop lights and few vehicles. The old stores looked too dilapidated to be quaint, and there is only one hotel, The Molokai Hotel. It took about two minutes to drive from the pier to the hotel comprised of several Tiki huts.

While checking in the open air lobby, a very beautiful Hawaiian woman told us about the manager's welcoming party that evening, and if we had any questions, just ask.

The lanai off our room faced a quiet inlet bay about 15 feet away. We had our own hammock and every morning I fetched papaya and fresh baked goods from the outdoor lobby to bring back to eat while we watched the fisherman go out with their nets. In the evening the flames of the tiki torches reflected off the water as we listened to the strains of guitars and ukuleles nearby.

Although the Hawaiian travel book didn't mention any restaurants there were a few excellent ones on this small island. The Cookhouse stood in the middle of what was once an pineapple plantation. (The pineapple industry has moved to Viet Nam.) The Cookhouse had six tables under the roof, and more picnic tables outside. There were no panes in the windows to keep the sudden down pours of rain off the food, but it was delightful and fun. Hawaiian style cooking features lots of sticky rice and fresh fish. The Paddler's was close to our hotel and was covered with a big palapa with no sides attached. Waiters took turns waving Palm frowns to keep the flies at bay. On our second trip to the restaurant, the manager greeted me with a kiss on the cheek and a handshake for my husband. We had observed this kissing and handshaking as a native greeting among locals and were flattered to be included.

The islanders still sing in the old Hawaiian language and most play instruments and dance the Hula. We followed the musicians where ever they played, The Coffee House, the hotel or Paddler's. It doesn't take long to become familiar with the whole island. the beaches, the hikes to waterfalls and rain forests. After dinner we would venture to the end of the pier and watch sun magically change the sky from blues to orange, magenta, pink, yellow, then to ink blue as it dropped into the ocean. We became immersed in the people, the scenery and the music of this magical isle.

Although remoteness was on the top of my list, Molokai

is not as easy to get to as Idyllwild. I may never return, but it will always remain a favorite place. When I told my friends we went to Molokai, I got the same reaction as I did when I mentioned Idyllwild. My explanation was simple, I like the remoteness, friendly people, scenery, good tasting food and the music.

Noreen Lawlor

Drought in Joshua Tree

where average rainfall is four inches
in the past year, we have had less than one inch.

The last time I saw rain was October in Bangkok.

As I walk from my hotel to the tourist boat
it starts to rain, a soft warm rain. I want to cry for
the preciousness of it. In the small green pond
the water lilies stretch out their long stems,
reach up their heads to receive it.
I open my mouth and let it slip down the back of my throat.
The brown river swells
floods turn everything on its banks
into mud and rust

Noreen Lawlor

Ghost Wind

We are having another big windstorm it knocked over my ugly man cactus, ripped apart my large potted chrysanthemum (the one I poured about a ton of water into and was just ready to bloom) and it is still whistling down the chimney.

All last night it blew gusts and bangs, sounded like it pulled off the roof (probably lost a few shingles) and right now it feels like it may blow through tonight. Funny when other people talk about high winds, I think, you should live where I live, buddy.

My son and I christened this place Rigel 12, after an old Star Trek episode about a planet that was always so windy you could hang your pots and pans outside to be sandblasted clean. I wish this was a rain storm but at this rate we would have floods.

I named this storm ghost winds because it heralds Hallow-een (Samhain), All Hallows Eve. The veil is thin these nights, moans and sighs of ancestors, long forgotten Celts' impris-oned song, a haunting wind. My thirty years' dead father keens Tura Lura Lura.

Wild wind whispers
song of the gone
where are you
come home Johnny
it's Samhain

Mojave Haibun

Here in the western Mojave we get wind storms instead of rain. This one blew in hard, bent the Joshua Tree in my front yard almost in half, scattered the last of its heavy white blooms. It brought sand like heavy mist that blocked out the mountains but at times the sky was that clear blue, so that you kind of had to wrap your mind around the contrast, bright sun and the gale force winds. It has a surreal effect, shifts your consciousness. Here, the wind has a persona.

Wild West cowboy wind
riding my Joshua Tree like
breaking a bronco

Caught in a killer sand storm on the 10 freeway between Palm Desert and Desert Hot Springs (a distance of maybe ten miles) I can not see more than three feet in front of me. The sand pelts my car in sheets like heavy rain or more like hail. I drive blind and hope the rest of the traffic will take it slow. Motorcyclists are off their bikes and hunker down under overpasses. To the north, the San Jacinto Mountains are obliterated and when I finally catch a glimpse of the sky it is a yellow polluted haze.

Sand twister flinging
handfuls of crushed saints
hurl dervish prayers

Richard Mozeleski

The 2013 Mountain Fire: The Lost Week

Lazy Monday morning-just got back home from somewhere, just a nice sunny day. Phone rings, it's my brother, hey, I'm in Hemet and the road's closed up to you, something about a fire up there. Really, where? Well, we can sure see smoke from down here. "Really"?

Walking back out the door I'd just entered five minutes earlier, my heart jumps a beat! This is what I've always worried about, and what could be possible. It was a recurring thought, but usually put back in the denial department of my brain. I said, "I'll call you back".

I called my friend Rick, whom I just left from in town. He lived between me and the "Plume" in the sky. Matter of fact, it looked as if he was about under it. Hey Rick, go outside and look up. What do you mean? You ain't gonna believe it, there's a fire by you and it looks big! Oh my God, I just walked in and didn't see anything. Where is it? From my point it looks like you're almost in it. It looks like May Valley, he says. Rick knows the mountains like a dog his yard. He's biked every trail up there.

I said," Let's go, I'll be over in two minutes". We shoot over to Cowbell Alley and get up on the ridge to see what is turning in to a war zone. Helicopters and planes are bombing this, what seems, a not so big fire, in perspective to the huge landscape before us. Our feelings are, they're pretty serious, they have got a handle on this. There was no personal urgency to the moment. The fire was just coming to the heliport for Mercy Air and it was interesting how , the fire crews, were taking a stand for the location, though in my estimation, the flames were 30+ feet high, and I wondered just how long the crews would stay there. The winds weren't what I would consider horrific, in hindsight. I wondered later how much all the aircraft aided the fire, hopefully just a misguided thought. The fire path was narrow and all seemed manageable. Where we were watching from was beginning to get pretty crowded with trucks and jeeps of people and I began to get concerned about being able to get out. Then the fire trucks started coming up the road and my concern level heightened. Hey Rick, can we drive down this road and get out of here? No, it's a locked gate at the end. We better go then. My vision of all these trucks trying to turn around on such narrows was a recipe for "not so good soup", let's go.

We got my Cherokee and drove down Cowbell Alley road a few hundred feet to a spot we could turn around, and not a moment too soon, for just as anticipated, it got frantic. Bigger trucks than ours trying to squeeze down the narrow road to do the same as we were, with fire crews behind them to make us, (meaning me), feel like maybe this is not one of my prouder moments, of being a looky loo. We got out of there and headed home with the thought of this thing will be contained before the sun goes down.

Well, that didn't happen and a little later back in town, from the post office parking I was amazed to see things were looking all the more serious. As curious lookers would walk in to the post office to get mail, all had about the same thoughts, is it going away from us? And in my newly acquired expertise of fire prediction, earned by my novice 2 hours observation training school, I said yes, no worries here. The fact that the planes were now getting what seemed as right on top of the lower end of south ridge was disconcerting, at best, and I thought to myself, you shouldn't lie to older women like that. I really wondered if it was going to come over into Idyllwild right there, but as it turned out, the smokes huge mass made it seem like it was closer than it was. It turned out the fire was heading towards others who weren't, I'm sure, talking like some guy in a bar watching a fight- they were getting ready for, or were already in one. The stories later would be heard about those folk trying to get horses, dogs, cats and kids out of hell's fury that was rolling towards them, as if it were a movie, a bad, bad movie.

It's still the first day and Idyllwild is just a view seat, no smoke really to speak of in town, just a lot of neighbor to neighbor "what do you know" and the like. Meanwhile, 40 miles away down in Palm Desert, my wife says the smoke is right at the back door at the bank she works in on highway 111. That amazed me, in how fast that much smoke travelled that far. She would not be coming home this night, or any of the next five, for that matter. She would stay with a friend from work down in La Quinta, and would have to get some new clothes for work, a small silver lining in this disruptive situation, for her anyway. Guys can wear the same clothes three days in a row, and think these things are just getting comfy, before the wife says the proverbial "are you gonna change your shirt today", and we always say out loud, "yes", but silently to ourselves, "and that's all", but I've digressed.

So into the first night, the story is of the fire lying down and is still pointing to an easterly direction. Idyllwild settles in. There are not a lot of full timers on my street, a ten room inn next door, empty. Marty, my other immediate neighbor, a mountain disaster prep guy, is very busy. The only other full timer, the fire commish lady, the same. So it's me and Holly whom for ten years now I thought was a chocolate lab, only to find out lately is a Chesapeake Bay retriever or something like that. Anyway, it's just us with no cable, but a thousand text messages from below. It was the So. Cal. story of the day, and would be for another week.

It was a long exciting and emotional day, fatigue was setting in and I still had a vintage box of 2013 cabernet, probably March, and it hit the spot just right. I thought about some of the kids camps back there in the path, and hoped that all went okay. I sat down on the couch, said some goodnights and a couple of I love you's, and then fell asleep.

Tuesday morning I came to understand the term "the fire is laying down", because it got back up and apparently it had got a good nights rest, it was on and moving towards the desert. As hard as that was to believe, they were afraid it was going to make it. Well, I don't really care much for that drive to there from here, and my wife even way less, since she does it five days a week. There's not a lot to burn after a certain point, and I'm not seeing it, I mean, if they can't stop it with what now looks like the army that went in to Kuwait, assembling to fight this thing. Anyway, that was the scuttlebutt for the next day or so, but then things changed as they are apt to in an area surrounded by desert, ocean, valleys and more mountains. The wind seemed to head back, and in our opinion, the wrong way, towards us.

The stories of several houses being run over down in the northern part of Garner Valley, were on peoples minds. We hear about a house fire here and there, now and then, bad wiring, chimney fire, a kid's mischief gone wrong, but not too often the term, "run over". Growing up in Orange County, since forever, I'm well aware of the "Santa Ana's" and I was cautious not to jinx the situation by even mentioning them and thereby waking them up from wherever they were, but I listened intently to any report of their lurking, and had not, fortunately, heard of any. To me, that was my indication of time to reevaluate everything. The fire had moved up the mountain, not that we could see, but smoke and ash we could.

Living up in Fern Valley, right below the Tahquitz Peak, and ironically, the fire tower look out, which I can see from my bedroom door, smoke, ash and embers were starting to come our way, which I'm sure the desert was glad to hear. The talk was now about evacuation. Wow, I thought it doesn't look that bad, but whatever, we will see. I have a decent feel for the geography, topography, the terrain up there. Fifty-five years old now, but probably the only reason we live here is from coming up as a young teenage boy scout. We would train up here, often getting ready for "summer vacation", a 70 mile hike in the Sierras. So, once a month we'd drive out to San Gorgonio or here to Humber Park, from Orange County on that two lane Santa Ana Canyon, past some race track and then down another two lane highway through some place called Sunnymead and a real live Air Force base, and then get ready to "throw up" on that winding, never ending road to some little town called Idyllwild, and then, in the dark, pull in to Humber Park where, with all the enthusiasm of a death row inmate taking the walk, strap on 40 pounds to 130 pounds of boy and get ready to walk up Devil's Slide, in the dark, which sucked ten times worse than in the light. Coming back to that trail thirty years later amazed me how the forest service cleaned up of an infinite amount of cobble, which I hated, to which today is quite comfortable. Anyway, up to skunk cabbage meadow, of which we could camp in those days, and lay our heads down, exhausted. From there, we would do ten miles of hikes, in a variation of ways, and then come back down on Sunday, which was, if possible, even worse Devil's Slide, pounding sore feet on all that loose rock, but then, as if it never happened, gleefully to the ice cream shop, for the cheapest reward for teenage torture, and that is why I live here now, its systemic, this place is hard to get out of you.

But the fire had moved in to the valley up there now, and that just could not be good. I could picture with a very unhealthy imagination what it was doing, a very sad thought indeed. That place is gorgeous, a perfect silence for the wind and the needle it whistles through. The last time I was up there, all the dead and down timber actually caught my attention. I did a no- no, and went cross country through an area I knew well enough so as not to worry, and was shocked by all the down timber, not realizing that would be part of the fuel for the "monster", a couple of years later.

The evacuation was on now. Marty, next door was not hesitating, what with five bulldogs, an interesting breed but a little crazy, it was a good idea. I don't know how he got them all in his truck, but I'm sure it would have made a good video.

The fire commish lady was packing up her rig like she'd won an Italy cruise, but had to be there in one hour. I was impressed how much you actually could get into one Bronco.

The Innkeepers didn't even say goodbye or go ahead and use the pool if you want, "I did". It was just me and Holly, wondering why this absolute "gotta go" command. I would get it later, but a rebel is a rebel and I, for this time, thankfully didn't get hurt.

I had no clue even what to pack. Truthfully, I was in a bit of denial. My friend Leigh has a list by her front door, which I found curious. She's an organizer's organizer. On that list are the top ten things you grab on the way out, no thinking necessary. Funny I thought back then, not bad I thought right now. I walked around thinking of what. Finally, I just started taking pictures with the cell phone of EVERYTHING and slowly, an item would stand out that should go. We don't have too many pictures of us, but enough and all special," in to the box". My wife collects books; I wouldn't know where to start. I collect cook books, I'll live. My son's high school varsity jacket hangs on a wall in his room he uses when home from college. As a kid I couldn't afford one, it was one of my proudest moments, getting that for him, "in to the box". My wife called, she has a drawer of special stuff in her small dresser, could I grab that? Sure. Two minutes later she calls back, could I just grab the whole dresser, sure. And on and on, this, that and this....All the bills on the desk, they'll be okay, they'll send new ones....some clothes, some food, some blankets. Were gonna need another car!

Earlier I went down to check on Jeff, he lives up here, but no car. I told him to pack, grab the dog and to my surprise, two cats, but what are you gonna say, and come stay, ready for the "you gotta go command". Darkness comes, fire lays down one more time, we're cool.

Next morning, dog, cats not happy, maybe best to take them back with Jeff to his place, but stay packed and ready.

I remember how the fire at our house in Murietta started

in front of the garage and was in the attic before we knew it, lost a car, but saved a son, it's all relative. So I started plugging every vent that could let any embers in and watering down and down and down, if that house could of grown, it would have. I was up there keeping the trees, plants, everything soaked. I'm still paying that water bill, "seriously". I was feeling pretty proud, this place was soaked, air tight, smoke and ash heavy outside, perfect inside. So as usual, when you get proud, you get stupid. Cooking lunch, Mexican burrito, flour tortilla on stove, one concussion too many "me" forgets, the tortilla is on fire and I can't open any windows. Sometimes God is too funny.

By now the calls and text are coming. Okay, "you need to go", and basically, you proved your point, "you're weird". But still no mention of Santa Ana's and each evening the dependable Hemet heat rises up the mountain and pushes up Devils Slide, and that in my mind, will keep the fire in the valley up there. Each evening I'd go up to my view spot up the road from the Creekstone Inn to almost the water tanks, a narrow one car width of drive, to a beautiful view of the saddle, and there I would appraise the situation for the night.

The fire on one night looked as if it was getting ready to show its face. At Wellman's Cienega, it seemed from down here it was ready to come over, but like the first day, when it seemed it was right over Rick's house, it was actually a bit away. I would swear I could almost see flames up there, but it would only be the mirage of light reflecting in the curtain of smoke.

The fire personnel and police were up there too. It was a good spot to reflect from, at one point, probably worn out from the long hours, I observed a curious situation. I was already past getting giddy and this was a perfect set up for one more silly moment. Two sheriffs had pulled in to the driveway below my look out rock and opened their trunk. Being how nobody was home, I became more curious and since they couldn't see me, I felt like a ten year old on a stakeout. All of a sudden, here they come, one of them carrying the loot to the trunk, acting as casual as one could. They were stealing pine cones...Flash, got it on the cell phone! My text with pictures "looters", ah, those city folks.

Next morning, fire crews are walking down the street and tagging each house for which ones were savable, most on our street weren't. They would note problems, where were hose bibs, was it cleared, etc. I thought it would be a perfect time to prank Marty and add to his list of violations for when he got back, but he never got to see it because the firemen politely removed them all before everyone got back in, damn!

For the next two days, Friday and Saturday, I could see trucks of young firemen headed up to Humber Park, knowing they were probably headed up Devil's Slide to do hand to hand combat. I wasn't sure, but what else I could not think of. That Saturday night, about one a.m., sleeping upstairs, I got up and looked out to see, just in case, if there might be any flames. Well, there weren't thankfully, but there wasn't a sound any where either, it was perfectly still, no wind, no lights, nothing. But there was a funny, unfamiliar buzz for one in the morning, "chain saws"....Chain saws? Wow, chain saws faintly from about two miles, as the crow flies, up in the valley behind the ridge, I pictured these young bucks with chain saws, and headlights strapped to their helmets. I had to stand there and make sure I was actually hearing that. I was amazed how much impact that had on me at that moment. All week, watching all the big wigs, all the pilots, all these cops everywhere, decently comfortable and here were these dudes and dudettes up there in the middle of the night, I was humbled.

And then, as if that wasn't enough, the good feeling got even better. At 4am Sunday morning, the sound of rain, as if to say from above, okay, that's enough, it's time to close it down. The peaceful patter of rain and the collective sigh of all who were here. It was a gloomy dark Sunday morning. The wonderful sound of rain, bringing with it the thought of families able to come back home. There would still be hesitation to open the town back up, but the floodgates would open and the "Idyllwild River" would rise again.

Firemen couldn't buy a drink, from coffee shops, to pick your favorite place. These guys and gals were the hero's we've known since we were kids. It was good to see, shoot, it was great to see. In our little corner of the world called Idyllwild, people were stopped to see precious that, that actually was, to put off the shelf of importance that, which never really was, and to be thankful for the simple truths in our lives that get "rolled over" by life.

Indian Canyons, South Course

for Ted

Sitting on the restaurant's patio, Ted's eyes flare.
His finger points, *Look at that bird.*

On the small tree emptied of its leaves, she perches
in front of the man-made pond near the 18th hole.

Her brilliant red-orange front blazes.
I tap a quick snapshot on my cell phone.

I promise to look up her name in my desert field guide.
On page nine, she poses next to her yellow-bellied brother.

Oh, vermillion flycatcher, what joy to discover what to call you.
Oh, Verizon smart phone, a smaller joy to have an app I am smart
    enough to use.

T Qi (Teresa Haliburton)

Displays

Poetry is in between
An English lesson
And a science project,

A mathematical link
To art and music;
Magical,

A place for
Ideas and sounds
To come together.

In song and dance
We act out
Our words and feelings

Deciding to what degree
We go public
Or private

With our displays
Of drama
Or comedy.

T Qi (Teresa Haliburton)

Earth and Fire

In between Georgia O'Keefe
And Van Gogh
I paint these flowers
I want to know.
The brush strokes are different
Intention is clear
I created a picture
Of something held dear.
Each piece is a variant
Held on a plate
And during the process
I can hardly wait!
To service others
Is my goal.
Now I can do it
From a beautiful bowl.

T Qi (Teresa Haliburton)

Found Pen

Free flowing
Free as silk

A pen's ink is
Like Mother's milk

Words on paper
From the heart

A skill practiced
Becomes an Art.

T Qi (Teresa Haliburton)

It's Me T Qi

Raised on Disney
And Dr. Seuss
Wonder why I
Take rhymes for use.

Sunday morning
And poetry
Made a mystic
Zen hillbilly.

T Qi (Teresa Haliburton)

Nature

Green trees
Golden leaves
Still silence
Rustling breeze

Healing spaces
Private places
Quiet movement
Balanced basis

T Qi (Teresa Haliburton)

Summer Sense

Pine needled and
Oak leaved trees,
Granite boulders
Still feel the breeze.

Butterflies flutter,
Squirrels chatter,
Bees sting.
What does it matter?

T Qi (Teresa Haliburton)

Three Rs

In 1948, a new marketing campaign
		Discard Today
Said we don't need to use again,
		You can throw these away

Plus, disposables are better
		We did as we were told,
Until 1970
		When landfills overflowed.

Then, begin again
		To stop earth's abuse
With the age-old ad:
		Recycle, Reduce and Re-Use!

T Qi (Teresa Haliburton)

Unique Liberty

The latitude and longitude of our lives
But for uniqueness, we're like bees in hives
Lilting laughter and loving of the living
Squarely sitting here now and giving
The fruits of one's labor kept on page
Rambling musings of a young old sage

Bit by the bug long before, but
Some time passed before the score
Began little by little to keep track
And remember all the back
*His*tory and *Her*story beautifully combined
To convey information of a feeling kind
Energy is moved and so are we
Conducted towards our own liberty.

T Qi (Teresa Haliburton)

Up A Tree

A symbiotic relationship with trees
        As humans, we have one of these
A growth that knows how we feel
        Mirroring ourselves back, is the deal,
Showing us the condition of our earth
        We should be promoting life by our birth.

The signs are clear, the destruction is done,
        The answer is action taken by one.
A person, a family, your neighborhood,
City, county, nation can help and could
Make a change for the betterment of being:
        Help everyone see what they're not seeing.

Creatrix

There is asymmetry
In what I do;

I can't say exactly
But know it's true,

With every creation
That I do make

There is some elation
For Heaven's sake!

To go through this process –
Sometimes Ordeal –

Okay, I'll confess
To me it's real,

An event, song or thing
From virtual non-existence

To this world I can bring
With a bit of persistence.

Marsha Schuh

510 Broadview

January seventeenth and minus ten,
Illinois' year for blizzards and pile-ups,
spinouts on neighbors' lawns.
Driving alone in the snow-blanched night,
delivering laundry in his truck with no doors,
Dad lost control, then seized control.

In less than two weeks, we backed down the drive
in our hawthorne green, fifty Ford ,
pulling an orange and white U-haul
packed with all we could take of our life—
mom's maple table and "mummy chairs,"
wrapped in rags to protect their polished grain.
and whatever else could be wedged in a four-by-eight
box on two wheels. Then on the road again
to my father's dream of a Promised Land,
flowing with orange juice, sunshine and waves.
"Things will be better starting today."
I believed what he said, for he was my dad.

We left Don Witty, whom I adored
as only an a girl of eleven can love—
he could outrun me and wrestle me
off the monkey bars, and best all,
his father owned Witty's Ice Cream Parlor.
Left my best friend Marsha Jones, Marsha the Two-th,
for I was Marsha the One-th.
Left Lucy Robinson, my "frenemy" from school
and Broadview Avenue. Sadly,

left our thirty-two Chevy, three-window coupe
that could never repeat the very same trip
it had taken but six years before.

Each of us was allowed two treasures.
My brother, a Tonka truck and Tinker toys;
I, my Nancy Drew books and trumpet;
and Mom, family photos, red crystal goblets.
Dad said, "You three are all I need."
But at the curb, he slammed on the brakes,
jumped from the car and into the snow,
ripped from the oak tree the address sign I'd made
in my fifth-grade woodshop for girls. "And this."

Aspen Glen outside Bishop, CA on Highway 395

The air is filled with saffron light
in this living room where I am safe.
I stand in the sunlight motes,
particles of air lit from within,
glistening amber flecks. The ground
shines yellow, trees breathe yellow, trunks
reflect a glow from above and below.
I smell the earth's musk of decay
swept under the gold leaf carpet.
The breeze whispers its solitary sound,
rustling the canopy of autumn aspen,
their leaves pirouetting above my head.
Leaves, clearing floor, air,
and my blond hair swirl together
in the dappled woods around me.
As the circle of trees sway,
I move, swept along in the dance
I'm only beginning to learn.

Marsha Schuh

Carob

The great green carob tree on Columbia Avenue
spreads its limbs across the neighbor's yard and drive.
Massive surface roots buckle the sidewalk,
their strength drawn from unknown depths.
The tree has grown in seventy years
to this mighty stature, its gnarled trunk
hiding the red wood heart,
now exposed by a broken branch.
Though broken, it blesses everyone
with fragrance and health.

The strain of its struggle against wind and rain
are revealed in the sinew and muscle of a torso
so wide it would take a small family to encircle it,
as they give thanks for shade, bird choirs, crunch
of pods beneath generations of feet and wheels
that release the fragrance of St. John's bread.
In autumn its flowers fill the air with paradox—
cadaverine odor of decay mixed
with the earthy smell of regeneration.

The seedpods ripen in summer
and the neighborhood revels
in the all-pervasive aroma of this tree
of many uses – aphrodisiac, unit of weight
used to measure purity of gold and gems,
natural sweetener, syrup, medicine,
and health food through the ages
from Gilgamesh through John the Baptist

and on to the present day.
How deep its roots must grow
to become so much more than itself.

Marsha Schuh

Everything I Need to Know about Men I Learned at Band Camp

Sometimes, boys at Arrowbear Music Camp chose a girl they thought was prettiest during the two weeks everyone would be together, and she became the girl of the fortnight.

Sometimes band kids were kind of nerdy, but these eight boys belonged to a club called The Cynics and wore light blue sweatshirts with a capital C, an arrow cutting downward through it.

Sometimes—once—one of them chose me, and he was the best horn player I ever heard, except Dennis Brain, but he was famous; besides, he'd never met me and he was at least 40, ancient.

Sometimes Jack wore dark rimmed glasses like Buddy Holly and when he flipped his long hair out of his eyes, he seemed much older than the 15-year-old boys I knew—maturity, a plus.

Sometimes, he quoted Shakespeare, Kerouac, and Kafka as easily as my father quoted scripture and with a passion for the word I'd never heard from anyone else, including my dad.

Sometimes, he led me to imagine things I'd never thought about—like what it would be like to kiss his lips, and stuff involving tongues. It was hard to concentrate on notes or counting rests.

Sometimes I forgot the boy back home who had never even tried to kiss me though we spent hours parked in his father's car, listening to KFWB channel 98, outside my house.

Sometimes, Jack caused me to do things that excited yet frightened me, like sneak out to Happy Gap
alone, talking, holding hands, cuddling till midnight.

Once, when we tiptoed back from Happy Gap after curfew, he kissed me in front of the girl's dorm. I thought it was true love.

Once warm honey ran through my body and my eyes closed, so I didn't notice the spotlights that came on – caught in front of the whole, entire camp.

Sometimes, I still want to believe like that.

Like That

Some of you remember riding in a station wagon
before there were seat belts
and the only thing protecting you
from harm was your mother's arm
and those trusty Chevy brakes.

Sometimes life is the station wagon
that brakes so hard it sends
you through the windshield
because her arm is no longer near
or strong enough to save you.

David Stone

A Glaucous Taste

purple-stained fingers cradle a silver spoon over
blackcaps and Wonder Bread ripped to cubes
mounded in a blue plastic margarine bowl
sprinkled with white sugar half submerged
in whole milk just poured from the rectangular
half-gallon glass bottle reflecting my sister's
chestnut braids ending in green yarn bows
fuzzy as the blackcap's leaves gray underside
opaque as the berry's tarnish lighter than
the patina that prevents my own face
from appearing in the bowl of my engraved heirloom
utensil as I consider how my grandfather
could possibly have had it sweeter   than I

David Stone

Getting Paid

I felt the pleasure of a finished job
when I grasped both dimes and the nickel
my Uncle Al paid for shoveling his walk.

I turned from his storm door to step:
the wind swept a fresh coat over the flagstones.

As clear as my frozen sigh falling before me,
I saw most work is never really finished.

I knew the snow would melt in April,
but there'd be crab grass to pull
from the cracks by the middle of May.

David Stone

Indian Corn: *Zea mays indurata*

Part the parched husks of autumn,
feel the season's flint, dentless pearls;
see Mississippian's calico maize—
ghostly white, bruise blue,
flame yellow, cockerel red—
survivor crop of Vermont's
year without a summer,
Algonkian's *uskatahomen*
shortened to hominy, ground
to grits, bound as ornament
of table, porch post, and door,
America's enduring native corn.

David Stone

Crane Tower's Squirrel-Style Fish

Wide-eyed as a squirrel,
the clever chef discerned
the emperor in disguise.

He'd heard the chatter:
Qianlong had journeyed
south along the Yangtze.

He'd chosen the Crane Tower
to try the local cuisine,
famously slightly sweet.

But just inside the door,
Qianlong's eyes caught
a perch before a seat.

The fresh offering
bounced on the altar
table, reserved for the gods.

The emperor insisted,
this was his dinner.
What was sin to him?

The frenzied chef
cut off the fish's head,
setting it to the side.

He scaled and gutted,
the Mandarin,
a fate he feared himself.

He scored its flesh back
and forth, leaving its tail,
never cutting its skin.

Needing more time,
He marinated the fish
in salty wine.

Lifting the fish
from its last brine,
he knew his pickle's fix.

Dust it in starch,
dip it in oil,
cover it in red.

He'd found the sweet
out of his sour fate:
serve the fish as squirrel.

David Stone

I'd Rather Be a Pie

I fear a jack-o-lantern's death:
a knife-piercing craniotomy,
a hand-swiping hysterectomy,
a thumb-pushing eye-gouge,
an amateur tooth extraction,
sodomy by candle.

Yes, I'd only need to grin
and bear one cauterizing night,
but I've seen how I'd be so
molded and collapsed on the stoop
in a week I'd be shoveled,
flipped in the dumpster,
forgotten in the fascination of
November's favorite pie.

Frances J. Vasquez

Golden Hoops

A Pantoum for My Nana Francisca Valenzuela

She always wore her enormous golden hoops
Sus arracades de oro – brillan como siempre
They glistened on ancient ear lobes like lunar appendages
Nana's pair of hoops dangled on delicate skin so transparent.

Sus arracades de oro – brillan como siempre
I anticipated they would tear through Nana's ancient lobes anytime soon
Nana's pair of hoops dangled on delicate skin so transparent
My cupped hands would catch the coveted earrings.

I anticipated they would tear through Nana's ancient lobes anytime soon
In the morning sunlight I glanced to see if this would be the day
My cupped hands would catch the coveted earrings
Nana's pair of hoops dangled on delicate skin so transparent.

In the morning sunlight I glanced to see if this would be the day
Today may be the day Nana's golden earrings would break through
Nana's pair of hoops dangled on delicate skin so transparent
She always wore her enormous golden hoops.

Today may be the day Nana's golden earrings would break through
Looking up to her adoringly, I sat ready
She always wore her enormous golden hoops
Should her earrings tear through, I sat ready to catch the treasure.

Looking up to her adoringly, I sat ready
She always wore her enormous golden hoops
Should her earrings tear through, I sat ready to catch the treasure
She always wore her enormous golden hoops.

Frances J. Vasquez

My Body Remembers

(Inspired by Vibiana Aparicio-Chamberlin's, "El Parto,"*
a late-20th Century woodcut on exhibit at Riverside Art
Museum, Fall 2013)

I remember – my heart remembers
new life growing inside of me
    una nueva vida creciendo
    dentro de mis entañas.
Deep within my core
my body,
my heart and soul
reminisce, recollect
    a babe developing:
    Mijo.
Movements memorized:
    the sudden jolts,
    flailing of limbs,
    gentle, subtle quivers.
My spirit danced with the rhythms,
    a waltz of creation, of growth
    we swayed, swung, whirled
    in pace with my *Mijo's* movements.
El crescendo de sus llantos; sus suspiros
    his whimpers; his sighs.
The passing of years, decades; my mind replicates
still
    the spasms of my crescent, waxing
    cradle.
Soul ignited. Awakened
Memory rekindled.
My heart recalls:
    I already loved him.

Mi corazón, mi carne recueredan los movimentos
        el cariño, el amor,
        el milagro dentro mi vientre
The miracle, the viscera of birth
        Con todo mi corazón
        con toda mi alma
My entire being - my body remembers
Forever.

*Spanish for "The Childbirth"

Frances J. Vasquez

Homage to Mark

The small front entry alcove serves as the main portal to our home. It is decorated with familial love and memorabilia: *familia. Amor y mucho cariño*. It features an eclectic array of sculptures, flowers, potted plants, solar lanterns, candles, rocks, polished stones, whimsical animal characters, and a vintage statue of *San Francisco de Assisi*. It is surrounded by faux birds and other animal creatures. For most of the year, a Christmas wreath adorns the front door. Frequently, the wreath was formed of fresh Pine boughs shipped to Riverside from an Oregon Pine tree farm. The Pine fragrance permeates our home's entry for a couple of months beginning in December. Then, it becomes a dried wreath - still pretty. To me, the wreath connotes the spirit and joy of *familia - Feliz Navidad*. For months, it serves as a visual aide to happy holidays. I usually replace it with something colorful during the summer. Or, Fall.

It was not always decorated in this manner. Losing my adult son Mark to a tragic vehicular accident left a profound void. His sudden death in 2006 devastated our family. It shattered my heart to lose my middle son. It changed us in many ways, and in how we go on with our lives. *Mijo* loved life. He was very popular, jovial and much loved. Music was his passion. He played Bass guitar with several bands: Punk rock and classic rock groups. Mark's passing made an indelible impact on how our family perceive and appreciate the pivotal aspects of life: how we enter and leave our lives. And, the key moments in between the beginning and the end.

In years past, the front entry would usually be decorated only during special holidays that our children enjoyed

- like Christmas, Halloween and Easter (in that order). Sometime in mid-December during the Christmas season, I would place a large decorated Evergreen wreath on the front door. I removed it soon after the Feast of the Epiphany on January 6 (*Día de los Reyes Magos*). An old standby was a gaudy Plaster-of-Paris Santa Claus and Rudolph the Red-Nose Reindeer figurine from Tijuana. I purchased it from a street vendor at my eldest granddaughter's insistence during one of our return trips to Rosarito in Baja California. While waiting in line at the Border crossing, our six-year old Marissa couldn't resist the vendor's persuasive sales pitch. She pleaded with me to buy it for her. I still recall her dramatic pleas, "*Please, Nana, buy me the Santa. I really, really want it! Please!" Díos Mío*, how could I negate her the statue.

For many years, we used to put out colorful strings of lights and other Christmassy decorations to please the kids, and to be in the spirit. At the end of the season, we promptly removed all of the decorations and carefully stored them for the following year. The front entry was essentially bare for most of the year. The Stucco wall on the right side of the entry used to support a United States Postal Service mail receptacle. Now, it holds two tropical Bromeliads mounted on ornamental driftwood. Indeed, our entire entry way used to be very utilitarian. Uncluttered. Simple. Service-oriented. Easy to enter - easy to exit.

The former easy-in and-out entryway gradually evolved into a permanent decorative homage to Mark. It began with the bronze "Guitar-Man" metal sculpture. My sister Lola saw it at one of her favorite shops. It immediately reminded her of her nephew Mark. She intuitively knew that I would like it. So much so that I've kept it on a special place on the right hand side of the entry near our home's front door. To display this new artistic figure, I relocated a small round metal table that had previously held a house plant. Mr. Metal-Guitar Man greets everyone who arrives at the front door - the main portal to our home.

Another item I found one Saturday while shopping at a Downtown Riverside antique store, was a vintage *San Francisco de Assisi* garden statue. It was weathered and faded. The paint had chipped exposing the grey cement foundation. I like its shabby chic look. I've moved it to several spots near the front entry. Eventually, I purchased a pair of matching wrought iron stands to display the modern Mr. Metal-Guitar Man sculpture next to the vintage San Francisco statue. The old and the new co-exist beautifully: *lo nuevo conviviendo con lo viejo....*

Flowers are a vital component to our homage. When in bloom, I offer bouquets of the vivid red "Don Juan" rose bush I planted in my *Mijo's* honor. Seasonal potted flowers add decorative flourishes: white lilies at Easter, yellow Marigolds for *Día de los Muertos* in November, amber Chrysanthemums at Thanksgiving, and red Poinsettias at Christmas. Flowers of each season are displayed in floral vases or recycled glass votive candles. Our favorite containers depict *Nuestra Señora de Guadalupe y el Ságrado Corazón de Jesus.*

Halloween is replete with pumpkins, skeletons, and Autumn colored candles. For patriotic holidays like Independence, Memorial and Veterans Days, the alcove and plants are festooned with American flags. Years ago, I purchased a large hand painted *Tonalá*-style pottery planter in Rosarito. The planter was formerly part of our living room decor containing tall stately palm trees. It's now a focal point of the front entry and contains lush offspring of my mother-in-law's variegated spider plants.

I installed a small, narrow metal bench to showcase gifted houseplants, and other treasures: rocks and polished stones; *a Nacimiento,* or Nativity niche during Christmastime; decorative sculls *(calacas) para Día de los Muertos;* and photo images of Cesar Chavez in honor of his birthday in March, decorated with grape clusters. What began as a very personal, private homage to Mark has evolved into a quasi-public altar for my *Mijo* and other special persons.

Various places in front of our home space are etched by unforgettable indicators of Mark's existence. It's as if *Mijo* wanted us to know that this is where he belongs. Here is where he will be lovingly remembered. Our front sidewalk and street curbs showcase concrete etchings he made as a youth in 1981, 1982, and 1984. Mark carved his name at two locations on the concrete street curb under the canopy of our mature Shamel Ash tree. He dated them "81" and "82." He autographed the sidewalk along the front lawn in "84." His high school buddies Pat and Matt denoted their symbolic presence, too. Curiously, for some unknown reason (to me), an etching along the street curb beneath our Ash tree states, "Where's Darin?" another of Mark's childhood friends. Yes, Darin, where are you? Do you know where Mark is?

To be sure, Mark's youthful 1980s concrete etchings on our street curbs and sidewalk were a prelude to our commemorating him. These set the stage for his remembrance. The very personal visual memorials, embellishments and decorations have developed over time as an eclectic homage to *Mijo*. A door is a metaphor for many things: Hope. Opportunity. Invitation, when open. Mystery, when closed. In ancient Egyptian and Greek architecture, the construction of false doors was a common element in a tomb or dwelling place. The made-up door represented a door to the afterlife. It gave the spirit a special portal to Heaven. The threshold to our home - Mark's childhood habitat - evolved from a simple, utilitarian entry way, to a welcoming, even amusing portico for people to traverse through. I delighted when Maria, our mail carrier said, "You have such a happy place." She knows. She delivers the mail.

Jean Waggoner

Finned Memories

"Glug, glug," sing the fishies
and we all swim down
the gentle stream
pursuing their
mercurial scales,
their resplendent fins,
leaping for joy when they
appear out of wet space
to dodge an obstruction --
solid rock, limb, shoal or
outcrop of twisted root.

"Arf! Arf!" we bark
in communal delight ,
not quite language,
but we don't need
words to know
that we belong,
we are part of this clan
of mammals swimming our
sea, our source of movement,
food, strength, regeneration
and floating ecstasy.

Splash, Splash! we gyre
in convert with our
parent presence,

our guide and
protector, the
one to whom
we gravitate at the close
of light, surrendering our bodies
to the wet element that flows, turns,
forms rapids, calms and shines –
or to the shore, for rest.

"Hmmm, hmmm" we purr,
inspiring and releasing
dry fluid
above
and below
the rippled surface,
twirling in facile grace
forward/back, up/down,
straight/twisted, gyrations
in and out of wet/dry fluids
our elements, our world, us.

"What? Where?" the waking
spirit wonders at crepuscular traces of
pre-human fantasm,
of lush Riverside wetlands
somewhere east of Adams Street

from Arlington Av. to Mount Rubidoux,
where the "Yelp!" of the cave, the
"Yelp!" of before the cave and the
"Yelp!" of the universal life force
thrilled our brood.

Jean Waggoner

Interface

Gaps are opening
In the midst of things.
A parade of cars winding
down Highway 74 slows
to a frontal view of
Its red Chevy lead
('60s Malibu) and the
ascending driver looks
uphill past mountain ridges
into the clouds, where a spoken
memory pulls, just out of reach.
"Home," it hints, in a father's voice.

Gaps are widening
in the midst of things.
Ponderosas crowd the canopy
Above a creek side summer show,
Fiddle and bazouki
(Irish jigs, Borscht Belt style)
and the Idyllwild viewer turns
eyes left to walkers on the bridge;
then, rising higher, to the ridge line,
where trees become remembered trees
and a Cherry Creek haunting that claims,
"Those good days" in breezy sighs.

Gaps are lengthening
in the midst of things.
Whole nights are given over

to Denver dreams
and pre-Denver dreams
in scenes of Colfax and
Larimer Streets aided and abetted
by *On the Road,* parental musings
and childhood memories --
and down in the heart strings a
deep chord sings, "Call Shirley
again, before it's too late."

Mae Wagner

I Am The Color Purple

I am the color purple
in all its variegated shades
from the faintest wisp of lavender
to its deepest, darkest hue.

I am the color of nature's paintbrush—
find me in the sweet scent wafting
from the bouquet'd bush of lilacs—
or the first crocus of spring
that breaks the bitter cold
of winter's icy spell.
I am the deepest purple iris
framed by shadowed sheaths of green.

I am the robes of royalty,
and charity's hand-me-downs
that clothed those left in Katrina's wake
or Haiti's rumbling terror.
I am in the shadowed folds and layers of mountains
reflected in the rear-mirrored view.
I am the color of Alice Walker's novel
of pain endured and power realized.

I am the bruise that goes deep to the bone
by the blow I couldn't deflect.
And though the purple fades to shades of green,
the bruise remains, unseen.

Mae Wagner

Remembering Mike Cluff

One of the topics Inlandia workshop leader Mike Cluff gave us that Thursday night at the downtown Riverside Library was to write about how sometimes we get so distracted about something—either as a speaker or as a member of an audience—that we can't concentrate.

I was sitting just to Mike's left side as he described how, as a speaker, you might worry—is my fly zipped? Do I have something on my teeth? Do I have toilet paper stuck to my shoe or could it be stuck in my waistband, trailing behind me like a tail?

Soon, that inner worry is running parallel to your speech, threatening to derail it.

Or, when you are a member of an audience, you can be easily distracted and lose the thread of the speech when all you can think of is—his fly is unzipped. Or the ladies sitting at the table on stage must not realize that there is no tablecloth to curtain the front of the table and they sit with their legs wide apart under the table and revealing the color of their underwear or whatever…

Well, funny he should mention it. I was having a tough time concentrating that night myself.

Mike, bless his soul, was not the model of a well-groomed man. Flip-flops, sweat pants and a tee-shirt seemed to be his usual wardrobe choice.

I didn't know Mike well so I didn't know what his personal life was like—but I often thought, Oh, Mike, you need someone to lovingly tend to you and give you the once-over before you go out the door.

Well, that night, all I could think of—especially since

Mike brought the topic of distraction up—was the very obvious hair sticking out of his nose and his very uneven haircut. I often sat by Mike and, just as often, there was often something rumpled, amiss, or out of place.

What on earth could I write about? Never in a million years would I want to hurt his feelings! I couldn't write about *him*—yet, I had to suppress an inward giggle over his choice of topic that night.

Rest in Peace, Mike!

Mae Wagner

Thursday Morning: Distraction Number One

Thursday morning
so much to do
so many distractions—
making my coffee,
I stop to watch,
a hummingbird outside the window
darting from one feeder
to another.

And then,
there he is—
the bunny who magically appeared
just after Easter.
Did he adopt our back yard
or is he trapped
with no way out?
Again,
of course,
 I must stop to watch
from my kitchen-window view
as he nibbles on the grass
hopping from one area of delicacy
to another.

His puffy white tail
contrasts against the gray-brown of his fur.
Ears flicker transparent

as he hops from
sunshine to shadow.

Thursday morning,
so much to do—
I cannot fritter it away.
I begin to empty the dishwasher
keeping an eye
on my backyard bunny.
I turn to put the colander away
from last night's strawberries
that topped the biscuits
under the whipped cream—
And, in that instant,
he disappears.

Mae Wagner

Thursday Morning: Distraction Number Two

I must curl my hair
for the day that lies ahead—
a chore made less tedious
by classic country music
playing on the radio.

Until…
Sammi Smith sings
one of Kris Kristofferson's masterpieces—
Help Me Make It Through The Night
—and I remember…
Oh! How I remember
the lover who
did help me make it through
many a night—
and I have love for him in my heart
still.

Hair half curled,
my eyes meet my own
in the mirror
that reflects a me
much older than I was
way back then.
And,
for the moment
I am transported
to that time so many years ago…
And, once again,

I am lost
in remembering…

Oh god,
why can't I go back
so he and Sammi Smith
can help me
make it through the night
once again.

Biographies

Alaina Bixon is a freelance writer, editor and coach who helps clients take their work from first draft to book. She has led Inlandia Institute writing workshops since 2012. She is a principal of Tilton Bass Publishing, which will publish Terrence Tingle's book Irish Yankee: An Irish Immigrant's Journals of Service in the U.S. Military, 1916-1919. The book will be added to the collections of the Getty, the Massachusetts National Guard Museum and Archives, and several libraries. Ms. Bixon has written and lectured on pseudoscience, travel, food history, and hippie-era San Francisco gurus. Currently she is writing about her college years at MIT in the 1960s. She has been invited to attend the Room of Her Own writers' retreat in August 2015.

Celena Diana Bumpus, BA, AODA is CEO, Editor and Book Designer of three publishing houses. For the last three years, she has taught four ongoing creative writing workshops at the Janet Goeske Senior Center in Riverside, CA. Two classes are dedicated to the writings of USA Veterans and their families. She is the published author of the poetry collection, Confessions (1998, The Inevitable Press). Her personal essay was published in the textbook, Street Lit: Representing the Urban Landscape (2014, Scarecrow Press). Her prose and poetry have appeared in the following publications: 2012 Writing From Inlandia (2012, Heyday Books), Verse/Chorus: A Call and Response Anthology (2013, Scarecrow Press), 2013 Writing From Inlandia (2013, Heyday Books), Invisible Memoirs (2014, Memoir Journal), Orangelandia: The Literature of Inlandia Citrus (2014, Inlandia Institute), On the Rusk Literary

Journal (2014) and online at Pen 2 Paper (2014). Her website is www.islandsforwriters.blogspot.com. Please visit her profile for her social media links

Dr. Deenaz P. Coachbuilder is an educator, artist, poet and environmental advocate. She is a retired school principal and professor in special education, and a consulting speech pathologist. Deenaz's poetry, commentaries and essays have appeared in national and regional publications and poetry blogs in the U.S. and India. Her recent book of poems, "Imperfect Fragments," has been received with critical acclaim both here and abroad. Deenaz has exhibited her paintings in oil in diverse venues, including a solo show. Deenaz resides in Riverside, Seattle and Mumbai, India. She enjoys reading, travelling, gardening, going for long walks, family and close friends, staying involved in the Indian American community and the Zoroastrian Association of California. She particularly cherishes being a wife and mother, and a recent grandmother.

Carlos E. Cortés is professor emeritus of history at the University of California, Riverside. His most recent book is his autobiography, *Rose Hill: An Intermarriage before Its Time* (Berkeley, CA: Heyday, 2012). Other books include *The Children Are Watching: How the Media Teach about Diversity and The Making—and Remaking—of a Multiculturalist*, published by Teachers College Press. Cortés is general editor of *Multicultural America: A Multimedia Encyclopedia* (Sage, 2013), scholar-in-residence with Univision Communications, and Creative/Cultural Advisor for Nickelodeon's Peabody-award-winning children's television series, "Dora the Explorer," and its sequel, "Go, Diego, Go!," for which he received the 2009 NAACP Image Award. He also travels the country performing his one-person autobiographical play, *A Conversation with Alana: One Boy's Multicultural Rite of Passage*, while he co-wrote the book and lyrics for the musical, *We Are Not Alone: Tomás Rivera—A Musical Narrative*, which premiered in 2011.

Laurel V. Cortés: At 17, I went to Mexico City alone to attend the University of Mexico. The experience changed my life and, after majoring in Spanish and minoring in Comparative Literature at San Diego State University, I worked for 28 years at the University of California, Riverside, in – guess what? – the Department of Literatures and Languages. The job perfectly suited my interests, and it's fun now to do a bit of writing on my own.

Don Dietz is a retired high school teacher with a Master Degree in Industrial Education and Counseling. Not only has he become a Stained Glass Artist in retirement, but during summer visits to Idyllwild he has gotten inspired to do some writing and he is learning to paint while basking in the glories of Idyllwild.

Judith Wright Favor, granddaughter of Leo and Cordelia, was born in Portland and raised in the rain. The author is still soothed by gray skies, moving waters and fluid processes. Married at nineteen, love's flow took her to California to raise two sons and a daughter before divorce. She worked in adoptions, flew airplanes, piloted hot-air balloons and taught psychology and human sexuality courses. It wasn't until 1981 that she enrolled at Pacific School of Religion. She pastored United Church of Christ congregations in San Francisco until the ministries of spiritual formation and writing laid claim to her soul. Happily remarried, she and Pete live at Pilgrim Place in Claremont, California. Her heart is enriched by her work in spiritual accompaniment, teaching and contemplative writing. To hone her craft, she values critiques from skilled writers. To stay fit she hikes, swims, race-walks and practices yoga, qigong and contemplative prayer. For fun she plays in lakes, creeks and ocean surf. For inspiration she listens to poetry and choral music, worships with Quakers and converses with fascinating friends, family and grandkids.

Nan Friedley is a retired special education teacher transplanted here some 28 years ago from Indiana. She taught in Fontana, at the California School for the Deaf in Riverside, and most recently in Moreno Valley. A collection of her poetry was included in the 2013 Inlandia Anthology. Nan has been a participant in the Riverside Inlandia Writing workshop for the last year.

Françoise Frigola, a regular attendee of the Idyllwild Inlandia workshop, was born and raised in France. She writes spontaneously, often on current social issues. With an MA in transpersonal psychology she sees the astrological chart as a map of the person's psyche. For several years, she wrote a column on *Counseling Astrology* in Aspect magazine. She has a BS in Computer science and business administration and over 45 years of experience as a computer consultant. She is also an internationally exhibited and collected artist.

C.R. Hawk is a longtime resident of Corona, California. C.R. Hawk discovered creative writing in 2001 when she studied memoir writing at the UCR extension center and continues her work with local workshops such as Inlandia.

Sally Hedberg lives in Desert Hot Springs but enjoys her summers in Idyllwild. She loves to travel and going to the places that are off the beaten track. She is a journalist but likes the freedom of creative writing and the support of the Inlandia group in Idyllwild.

Noreen Lawlor is a poet who lives in Joshua Tree. The Mojave with its rocky desert landscape, remarkable creatures and weather have been a rich source of inspiration for her work. She is also a visual artist and frequently combines her poetry with her art. She has participated in the Inlandia writing workshops over the last several years. She holds a Master's degree from the University of Pennsylvania. Her poems have been published in various journals including "The Sun Runner Magazine" and in the anthology "A Bird Black As The Sun."

Richard M. Mozeleski is a retired Landscape Designer. He has been married to his wife Diane for 22 years, and is the father of Ian Mozeleski, a college Basketball player. Richard has coached local Basketball and Baseball players for the past decade and has recently taken up writing and theatre after moving to the picturesque town of Idyllwild, CA. Richard has recently begun a ministry to feed local homeless men.

Margie Norris retired to Palm Springs with her wife in 2005. They live in the desert for seven months and return to San Francisco for the remainder of each year. She has been writing poetry since her early thirties. She experiences the desert landscape and mountains as a constant source of serenity. Margie enjoys the diversity of inhabitants in the desert and the opportunity to develop solid friendships in this special place.

T Qi (Teresa Halliburton) has been a writer, artist, and educator for forty years. In Spring 2014, Idyllwild supporters sponsored a gallery for her work! In 2015, two local shows featured her poetry and art. T Qi was celebrated as one of the Wise Women of a Mountain Village and "Avatar's Enlightened Liberation" was published. The Town Baker's annual Box Show hung two pieces: "I Was Run Over By A Baby" and

"Just Monkeying Around". T Qi invites y'all to come up to the hill and write.

Marsha Schuh and her husband Dave are currently remodeling the 88-year old home in Ontario that they moved into as a young couple. She teaches English at CSUSB and is working on a collection of poems—inspired by her early morning walks—about Ontario and its history. Marsha's poetry has appeared in literary journals such as *Pacific Review, Badlands, The Sand Canyon Review, Shuf,* and *Inlandia.*

David Stone moved to Riverside, CA to attend graduate school at La Sierra University, where he met his future wife Cathy. He has taught English at Loma Linda Academy for more than a decade. David enjoys writing, cooking, and exploring nature in Redlands, CA with his wife and two children.

Frances J. Vasquez resides in Riverside. She has a diverse background in public service, and was the Executive Director of Other Cultures, Inc., an international student exchange program specializing in exchanges between Mexico, Central America, Canada, and the U.S. She attended Inland schools and graduated with BS and MBA degrees from the University of California, Riverside. An aficionada of arts and letters, Frances enjoys attending and organizing cultural events.

Jean Waggoner established Idyllwild's Inlandia Writing Workshop in the summer of 2010. A "freeway flier" with a Master's from CSU Fullerton, Jean teaches English and ESL at community colleges in Riverside County. Her work includes story-telling, essays, fine arts reviews, advertising copy and poetry that has appeared in on-line and print publications, including business journals, the National Poetry Anthology,

Phantom Seed and Inlandia publications. She has read poetry at Inlandia and Idyllwild community events and at the Poetry Week in San Miguel de Allende, Guanajuato, Mx. (Jan. 2009). Jean recently co-authored with Douglas Snow *The Freeway Flier and the Life of the Mind* (ISBN # 978-1-4568-3119-6 paperback, with e-book available at Amazon, soon).

Mae Wagner is firmly rooted in the Inland Empire area and sees Inlandia stories everywhere just waiting to be told. She says, "writing has always been a passion, but largely relegated to the back burner while I focused on raising a family, earning a living and going to school." Over the years, as a longtime Inland Empire resident, she has written for a public relations firm, the Riverside Chamber of Commerce; The Chino Champion newspaper, and had several columns published in the Op-Ed page of the Press-Enterprise when it was locally owned, including a column on the Stringfellow Acid Pits in Glen Avon, just west of Riverside. She currently writes a column for her home town paper in Hettinger, North Dakota and is enjoying being a member of the Riverside Inlandia writers workshop, which she has attended since its opening session in the summer of 2008.

About the Inlandia Institute

The Inlandia Institute is a regional non-profit literary center. We seek to bring focus to the richness of the literary enterprise that has existed in this region for ages. The mission of the Inlandia Institute is to recognize, support and expand literary activity in all of its forms through community programs in the Inland Empire, thereby deepening people's awareness, understanding, and appreciation of this unique, complex and creatively vibrant region.

The Institute publishes high quality regional writing in print and electronic form including books published in partnership with Heyday under the Inlandia Institute imprint as well as independent Inlandia Institute publications.

Inlandia presents free public literary programming featuring authors who live in, work in, and/or write about Inland Southern California.

We also provide Creative Literacy Programs for children and youth and hold creative writing workshops for teens and adults.

In addition, every two years the Inlandia Institute appoints a distinguished jury panel from outside of the region to name an Inlandia Literary Laureate who serves as an ambassador for the Inlandia Institute, promoting literature, creative literacy, and community throughout the entire Inlandia region. To date, Laureates include Susan Straight (2010-12), Gayle Brandeis (2012-14), and Juan Delgado (2014-16).

To learn more about the Inlandia Institute please visit our website at www.InlandiaInstitute.org.

Other Inlandia Publications

Independent Inlandia Imprint Publications

No Easy Way: Integrating Riverside Schools - A Victory for Community
Arthur L. Littleworth
Edited by Dawn Hassett
Foreword by Dr. V.P. Franklin
Introduction by Susan Straight

Tia's Tamale Trouble
Julianna Cruz, author
Tracie Lents, illustrator

Orangelandia: The Literature of Inland Citrus
Edited by Gayle Brandeis

Dos Chiles/Two Chilies
Julianna Cruz

2011 Writing from Inlandia: Work of the Inlandia Creative Workshops
Edited by the Inlandia Institute Publications Committee

2012 Writing from Inlandia: Work of the Inlandia Creative Workshops
Edited by the Inlandia Institute Publications Committee

2013 Writing from Inlandia: Work of the Inlandia Creative Workshops
Edited by the Inlandia Institute Publications Committee

Heyday Inlandia Imprint Books

Empire
Lewis deSoto (forthcoming)

Vital Signs
Juan Delgado and Thomas McGovern

Rose Hill: An Intermarriage before Its Time
Carlos Cortés

No Place for a Puritan: The Literature of California's Deserts
Edited by Ruth Nolan

Backyard Birds of the Inland Empire
Sheila N. Kee

Dream Street
Douglas F. McCulloh

Inlandia: A Literary Journey Through California's Inland Empire
Edited by Gayle Wattawa with an introduction by Susan Straight

Inlandia Electronic Publications

Inlandia: A Literary Journey, an on-line journal
Edited by Cati Porter

Audio Guide
Inlandia: A Literary Journey Through California's Inland Empire
Moderated by Gayle Brandeis

Inlandia Literary Journeys Blog
http://www.localauthors.pe.com

www.ingramcontent.com/pod-product-compliance
Lightning Source LLC
Chambersburg PA
CBHW060422260626
47161CB00005B/1739